Celtic Viking

Heart of the Battle Series, Volume 1

Lexy Timms

Published by Dark Shadow Publishing, 2015.

CELTIC VIKING
The Heart of the Battle Series
Book 1
By
Lexy Timms
Copyright 2015 by Lexy Timms

This is a work of fiction. Similarities to real people, places, or events are entirely coincidental.

CELTIC VIKING

First edition. April 12, 2015.

Copyright © 2015 Lexy Timms.

Written by Lexy Timms.

Also by Lexy Timms

Hades' Spawn Motorcycle Club
One You Can't Forget
One That Got Away

Heart of the Battle Series
Celtic Viking
Celtic Rune
Celtic Mann

Managing the Bosses Series
The Boss

Saving Forever
Saving Forever - Part 1
Saving Forever - Part 2
Saving Forever - Part 3
Saving Forever - Part 4
Saving Forever - Part 5
Saving Forever - Part 6

Southern Romance Series
Little Love Affair
Siege of the Heart
Freedom Forever
Soldier's Fortune

The University of Gatica Series
The Recruiting Trip
Faster
Higher

Stronger

Standalone
Wash
Loving Charity
Summer Lovin'
Love & College
Billionaire Heart
First Love

Heart of the Battle Series

Celtic Viking
Book 1
Celtic Rune
Book 2
Celtic Mann
Book 3

Coming June 2015

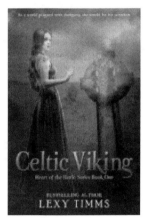

In a world plagued with darkness, she would be his salvation.

No one gave Erik a choice as to whether he would fight or not. Duty to the crown belonged to him, his father's legacy remaining beyond the grave.

Taken by the beauty of the countryside surrounding her, Linzi would do anything to protect her father's land. Britain is under attack and Scotland is next. At a time she should be focused on suitors, the men of her country have gone to war and she's left to stand alone.

Love will become available, but will passion at the touch of the enemy unravel her strong hold first?

** This is NOT Erotica. It's Romance and a love story.

* This is book 1 of a 3 book series *

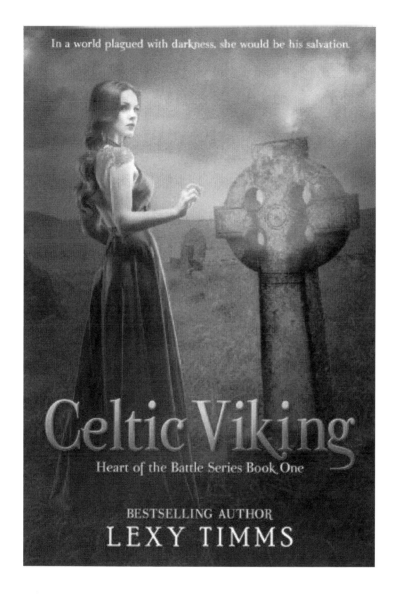

Chapter 1

Somewhere in North-East England

The fog hung in the air like a habit belonging to a monk, as if never meant to depart from the body. It was impossible to see more than twenty feet in front, or behind, or anywhere, as a matter of fact. The English could be standing in the middle of the field advancing and neither party would know until they bumped into the Saxon army. They'd been awake since dawn, but no one knew what time it was now because the grey clouds would give no hint of where the sun might be. The Saxons were willing to battle and die for this country?

Erik squinted, trying to will his eyes to see through the thick, smoky-grey mist. He imagined the field before him, without the fog, the lush green of the grass and surrounding trees. The land stood perfect for agriculture, not battle. He tried to keep his thoughts in check. At twenty, he should be home in Denmark, maybe farming but definitely married, with a slew of sons and some daughters. Instead, he stood here, in the cold, wet mud of this forsaken country. All his training and education made him an excellent military commander. Except he really just wanted a simple life.

"The men are saying King Halfdan's going to speak with us. He and his guards are coming up the rear of the hill," Marcus spoke, bringing Erik back to the present.

"King Halfdan? Who's calling him that now, cousin?" Erik kept his face blank, though his insides were boiling.

Marcus stood beside him, grinning. "I think 'tis safe to assume the rumor was started by the *king* himself. He plans to lead this Great Heathen Army to battle."

Erik glanced the small distance he could see in front of him and glared. His body stood erect and it took an effort to unclench his jaw. "We are not the Great Heathen Army. It's the Great Danish Army." He bit the inside of his cheek, tasting blood. "Halfdan will not lead us today. He's a man of words," Erik couldn't hold back a snort, "and smart enough not to risk his life to appear heroic in this bloody fog. He'll do as he always does; talk with the commanders, ride amongst the men and then hide behind the dog's tail."

Marcus sucked in his breath. "As much as you don't like the man, I suggest keeping those opinions inside your head, or in the privy of your tent. I know how you feel, cousin, but there are many who disagree."

"The man's a tyrant. His goal is to pillage and conquer as much of England as he can. He has no respect for the people who have toiled to make this land livable. He would prefer to kill and burn them all." He felt Marcus' elbow sharp in his ribs, even through his chain mail. He'd seen the carnage Halfdan had created throughout Europe. Fighting for him was not something he would have chosen.

"Enough! If your father heard you speak –"

"I'm sure he's turning in his grave. I know who my father was and what he wanted of me. I'm here, am I not? I'm still doing his duty, years after his death."

"At least try to enjoy it." Marcus meant well and Erik was fond of his younger cousin. Marcus had risen through the ranks, both on his own accord but also through Erik's guidance.

Erik also knew only he himself had the power to speak his mind, and none of the other commanders would challenge him. He may be one of the youngest leaders of the Saxons, but he'd been fighting and organizing battles alongside his father longer than he could remember. He had earned their respect.

A murmur began through the men. Erik heard the quiet talk before those ones in his line of vision started to form two lines, bending down to one knee. Marcus dropped down, his right hand making a fist and covering his heart. Erik reached to settle his brown Arabian mare, rubbing her nose. He would bow to no leader who called himself a king. Their king was in Denmark, safe in his castle.

Halfdan rode in on a large, white horse. Erik didn't understand the white horse. It stood out in battle, like a target. Maybe it would be best if the man stayed at the rear of today's skirmish. As much as Halfdan loved the kill and fight, he would be marking himself for certain death.

"Erik," Halfdan spoke, his voice raspy and deep.

"Yes... Sire," he added grudgingly. He met Halfdan's unwavering gaze with no fear. Halfdan's blue eyes were full of ice and hatred, even as he spoke among his own men. The two were the same height, but Erik was lean, muscular and all legs. Halfdan was broader shouldered, still fit but age had begun to creep up on him. He hid his slight belly behind the full-length, fur cape.

"Are the men ready to fight?" It sounded like he needed to clear his throat though the man never coughed.

"They are, but visibility's very limited. The fog seems to stay connected to the ground, refusing to dissipate."

Halfdan waved his hand as if swatting a fly. "It will sharpen the men's senses. They'll have to be thorough; any English man partially alive could kill them."

"Yes."

Halfdan glared at Erik and gave him a once over. "You're not afraid to die?"

"No."

"You're fearless. Maybe stupid, but the soldiers follow you and that's good enough for me. Lead the men today, and when the victory is done give me the credit. You'll be rewarded as per your station. Make an example to the rest of the people in this god-forsaken country."

Erik rubbed his mare's neck. The horse snorted and side stepped. Erik forced himself to relax and scratched the horse behind the ears, bringing her back toward him. He said nothing to Halfdan.

"The men may loot the nearby town afterwards. They can help themselves to any valuables, food or cattle." Halfdan turned to go but swung the horse back around. He stared at Erik, a dark smile playing on his lips. "They're welcome to anything, but warn them not to touch the women. Kill them. No touching or gratifying from our men. I'll put a sword to any of the men who do. We will not weaken our Saxon blood with this tainted, dirty race. No breeding, or death by my hand."

Erik swallowed, his throat now dry in the moist air. Halfdan's radical beliefs would be impossible to instill in the soldiers. Erik agreed with not touching the women but for entirely different reasons. They were not part of this war for land.

In order to prepare for the fight for the British island, the Saxons needed men, a lot of men. They took prisoners willing to fight and die for their freedom. Some of the men were decent but most fought for themselves, not their king and country.

On top of this, the men had been travelling for weeks with more time spent in preparing for battle. They hadn't seen, let alone been with, a woman in months, and for Halfdan to give them freedom to loot but not touch. Erik would have a bigger battle there than on this field.

"Is it understood?" Halfdan's raspy voice showed his impatience from Erik's lack of response.

"It'll be done, Sire," Marcus spoke, still kneeling on the ground by Erik. "I'll be sure and let the men know, and hold them to their word." He tapped his sword.

"Good. Get this battle done before sundown. I'll watch this one from the hill. This one's easy. Our next battle is critical, and I plan to be fresh to lead the men myself." Halfdan clicked his horse forward. "Erik, I expect a full report after." He turned and rode away, the fog swallowing him up.

Erik stood beside his mare, brushing dried dirt off her coat. He felt Marcus rise beside him and spoke, not bothering to look in his direction. "Do not tell the men they are free to loot but not to touch the women till after the fight. Some of our soldiers are short-witted and it will be enough to distract them from their duty. Let the combat finish and then tell them about their next charge."

"As you wish."

Marcus' curt reply had Erik turn his head in the direction of his second-in-command. Their mothers were sisters, but they looked nothing alike. Marcus had dark, curly hair and brown eyes. Erik's blonde, almost white, hair stood out on the battlefield like Halfdan's new horse.

Erik earned respect and loyalty. He knew his men would never forsake him. Marcus was different. He could command a group of men simply by the threat in his voice. When they played as lads, Erik often believed that Marcus could burn someone alive, simply by speaking.

"Don't be hostile with me, Marcus. I'm still above you."

"Fine, Sire. Might I suggest that you learn to reply to your king then, instead of leaving it to me?" Marcus stalked away toward his horse to prepare.

"He's not my king," muttered Erik. Lifting his chain mail shirt so it lay properly in place, he checked his clothing and gear. He'd sharpened his sword upon rising this morning. His axe had been sharpened the night before and he'd also attached his small, hand-size knife to the belt. It had been the last gift from his father, engraved on the handle by his mother.

He pulled it from his belt and held the handle, gazing at the knotted pattern and the name on the worn wood. He had been named after his father, Erik Jorgen. He could see the care his mother had taken to carve the pattern. He hoped to pass it on one day to a son. Turning it over, he noticed the red and brown stained into the wood. He meticulously cleaned it after each battle, but years of blood and gore had permanently stained the one side and found its way nestled into the carvings. It brought him back to the focus at hand.

The scouts had reported very little the days leading up the battle. They could find little information on the English army, almost like they were invisible. It made these grounds very deadly, for both sides. Erik would have preferred to wait, but Halfdan refused to stall any longer. He wanted to move toward Northumbria and capture the central waterfront shipping town.

Erik glanced around at the other commanders under him. The fog had begun to lift a bit, still thick, but he could now see fifty feet in front of him. It must be getting close to mid-morning. They needed to prepare to advance or all would be wasted another day.

A commander walked by, older than Erik by ten years but still under him.

"Johan, are the men ready to march?"

"Aye, Sire." He stood erect and faced Erik. "When would you begin?"

"Now. There is no need to wait or the day will be lost. Have the archers in front to hold the ranks. Hopefully, the heat from their fire will remove some of the damn fog. We'll advance on foot, and leave the horses until they're needed. Sound the warning. We march in half an hour." Let the bloodbath begin.

Chapter 2

872 A.D.

In the Southern Tip of Scotland

Linzi stepped out of the house, dashing away from the shouts of her father and brother. She didn't need to hear the argument that never ceased to bore them. If her mother had still been alive, she would have swatted both men on the back of their heads and sent them to their chores. Plenty of work on the small farm always needed to be done. Kenton, her brother, felt the need to join the English army to stop the vicious Saxons, but her father bickered back that he was needed on the land.

Once past the stone wall surrounding the house, she slipped her shoes on and headed west, toward the sunset. Less than a mile walk brought her to the small hill on the edge of their land. Lifting her skirt, she trudged up the hill and sat down on one of the flat stones near the small burial plot. Her mother, grandparents and a baby brother who'd died at birth were buried here. She sat facing west, her back to the graves but near her mother's resting place.

Inhaling and slowly exhaling several long breaths, she let her shoulders drop as she hugged her knees. She watched the pink sky with the amber ball make its way into the horizon.

"Those men will always be boys, Mother." She often spoke to her while she sat here. "They both refuse to listen to me, or each other. Kenton shouts about the need for blood-shedding to save our country and drive off the Saxons. Those horrible beasts kill for pleasure. I see his point in fighting for what is rightfully ours, but I don't want him to join you here on the hill. Let the others fight. When the wolf comes knocking on our door, then Kenton can push his cause."

Having said the words aloud, she no longer felt the anxiety tightening inside of her. She wished she could say the words to her brother. He was two years her elder, nineteen years old, and full of vigor. He needed to find himself a wife to focus his energy. Three girls in town are vying for his attention and Linzi wished he would just choose one and settle down.

Sighing, she stretched her arms out behind her, leaning to let her fingers curl around the soft, green grass. She closed her eyes to enjoy the last bit of warmth the sun had to offer before it disappeared. She needed to head back to the house and finish making supper. Her boys, as she called her father and brother, had been working hard in the fields. Spring had come early this year and with the soil soft from the rain, it had the boys hungry by dinner time. That was probably the reason behind their argument, they needed to eat.

Standing up, she brushed off the grass on her skirt and blew a kiss toward her mother. Making the sign of the cross, she straightened her shoulders and headed down the hill. She thought about what she'd need to say if the argument still lingered. She hoped they'd be finished but knew that was not likely. They were as stubborn as each other.

The house stood silent as she rounded the old stone wall. She smiled to herself as she remembered as a child asking her father how old the wall was. He'd simply replied, old as the hills, old as the hills. It always made her smile when she remembered the look on his face. He'd been so serious, with a slight frown and creased brow. Her mother had shouted from the door that his face would freeze if he kept the look. He had laughed and bounded up the walk to swing her around in his arms. He now had laugh lines around his mouth and forehead to disprove her theory.

Blinking to clear her thoughts, she glanced around the yard and noticed her father out by the horses. He appeared to be giving them a brush down and checking their hooves. Cocking her head slightly, she thought she heard him whistling. He never held a grudge or stayed angry. He fought with intensity, but he could walk away and leave the matter until it needed to be dealt with again. Unlike her brother, who couldn't seem to let things go.

The savory scent of meat cooking brought her attention back to the house. It also brought a rumble to her stomach. She hurried inside and slipped her shoes off by the door. Kenton sat at the table cutting the carrots and peeling a few loose leafs off the sprouts. He tossed them into a black pot every few moments.

"I've had enough of Brussels sprouts. I can't wait to have some peas, or even spinach. The east field is almost ready for seeds. Hopefully by tomorrow afternoon we can start planting." He glanced up and smiled.

"Are you cutting my vegetables as a peace treaty?" Linzi couldn't resist asking.

He shrugged as he tossed the last of the carrots into the pot, splashing some of the water out. "My argument is not with you. I just wish he," Kenton nodded toward the barn, "would allow me to go."

"Father's right. You know he doesn't disagree with your feelings that this land belongs to us. However, rushing out blindly now would only be foolish. The farm needs to be looked after and I need to be fed." Her stomach rumbled again as if to add a voice. She took the pot and turned to put it on the hearth to boil.

"You do need to eat. You're tall and too thin. Even that long red hair of yours looks dull. You're never going to catch the eye of a man if you don't look after yourself."

Linzi swung around, feeling her eyes grow wide. "I think you need to worry about your mate-finding before you start criticizing–" She stopped when she saw the smile on her brother's face and the laughter in his eyes. Seeing an uncut carrot on the counter, she grabbed it and drilled it in his direction. It hit him square in the chest.

"Ow! I take it back." He rubbed his chest, by his heart. "That's going to leave a bruise."

"Good," she laughed.

"Who taught you to have such good aim?" He pushed away from the table and stood. He picked the carrot up and started chewing on it.

"My big brother. I may be thin, but there's muscle hidden under this woman's clothing. Lean and mean." She checked the potatoes and noticed they were done. Grabbing prongs, she set them away from the fire. "Dinner's almost ready. Go wash up and tell Da' that he needs to come in as well." She saw Kenton's mouth tighten into a thin line. "Be nice," she warned, shaking the prongs at him.

He raised his hands in mock surrender, the anger leaving his face. He slipped out the back door.

Linzi heard the water from the pump splash into a bucket. She looked out the window and saw her brother's back facing the house. She slipped into her bedroom and pulled the small chest out of the cupboard in the wash stand. Sitting on the edge of her straw bed, she reached in to take out a sterling, ornate vanity mirror. Her father had bought it for her mother a million Christmas' ago. The silver in the mirror had faded in a few spots, but the beveled glass still showed her reflection. She stared at her brown eyes, the small spray of freckles across her petite nose. She had always liked her lips, similar to her mother's. The full pink never needed rouge or paint on them.

Small benefit, but they made the rest of her face appear pale. The cloudy winter months didn't help to add any color. Hopefully, the next few weeks of planting would help put some color and hide her freckles. She pulled her dark, red hair and angled the mirror to see how dull it really looked. Her brother was right. Maybe later this evening she'd cut a few inches off and give her hair a wash tomorrow after planting. No need to do it tonight as the dirt in the fields would find its way to her face and scalp even with a scarf tied around it.

She did want to look beautiful. She dreamed of catching the eye of a gentleman one day, and hopefully, not too far in the future. She wanted a husband and children. She just didn't know how to find someone she could love like her father had. The boys her age that she knew still seemed young. A few of her brother's friends were nice, but none dared speak much with her, for fear of riling Kenton's infamous temper. Maybe this summer things might change and she'd get a chance to meet someone special.

Low, angry voices and stomping feet coming from the kitchen brought her attention back to the present. She slipped the mirror back into the wooden carved chest and pulled her hair back to tie it into a bun. She ran the few steps down the hall and into the kitchen.

The angry voices turned to weather conversation when she entered. Kenton moved to the window and looked into the early night sky. Linzi rolled her eyes at both of them and went to set plates onto the table. She pushed her brother out of the way as she pulled the meat from the hearth. The mouthwatering smell coming from the beef had the two men sitting quietly at the table in seconds. Tossing potatoes and vegetables onto each plate, she then grabbed the pitcher of ale and set it on the table.

She swatted her brother's hand as she sat down. "We need to bless the food before you make a pig of yourself." She pulled her chair in and said a short prayer of thanks.

They ate in content silence. The hard work from the day and cool evening air seemed to create an enormous appetite in each of them. All the food disappeared into bellies. As Linzi began to clear the table, her father poured each of them a glass of ale. He leaned back in his chair.

"Your friend Darren rode by on horse when I was out in the barn before." Her father looked at Kenton as he spoke.

"What did he want?" Kenton took a long drink from his mug.

"He was heading into town but stopped by to mention that he'd heard that war was breaking out in the south. It seems a large fleet of Saxons is determined to make a stand again."

Linzi's heart fluttered and she spun around to watch her brother. Kenton set his ale down but did not look angry.

"Those beasts are going to massacre the towns down there. Our army is building in the Midlands. They aren't ready to do battle, nor will they be able to reach the south in time." Kenton shook his head, his chestnut brown hair falling forward to cover his eyes.

"Darren said something similar. Looks like their leader, I think his name is Halfman, is hungry for bloodshed."

"Halfman? Ironic that the Saxons would choose a commander by that name."

"Darren said that the man already calls himself the King of England."

"Bah." Linzi couldn't keep her disgust inside. "King of England? Britain has no father. Not from Rome or France or anywhere and this Saxon thinks he can step on our land and become our king? Shite!"

Kenton picked up his ale, but Linzi could see him grinning behind his mug. She was tempted to throw hers in his face. That would wipe the silly smirk off. She had every right to voice her opinion in this house. She opened her mouth to let him know her thoughts.

"Hold your tongue, Linzi," her father warned. He too had the corners of his mouth twitching upwards. "You're right to think that way, but you're also a lady, and there is no excuse for vulgar language."

"Sorry, Da'."

"Let's just pray the army in the Midlands stops them. Northumbria is a stronghold that the Saxons will want. That is no surprise. The ports and the farmlands are rich for trade and export. I can just imagine what'll happen if they sack the city." Her father picked up his ale and gulped the remaining down.

Linzi and Kenton both sat silent. Images of horror ran through her thoughts and she felt her brother might just be relieved that he hadn't joined the army – yet.

Chapter 3

"Hold the line!" Erik hollered to the commanders under him. They shouted the phrase down the rows to their men. Erik heard his words turn into a murmur as it reached the front lines. He stood amidst the bloodbath and carnage. The men did not need to hold the line for their safety, they were annihilating the English. He wanted the men to stay in rank to avoid more death and let the English retreat.

Marcus appeared at his side, still on horse. Erik looked up at his cousin as he sheathed the handle of his axe, but kept his sword in hand. Marcus and his horse were covered in brown and deep red blood. Some had dried from the early start of the battle, the fresh still dripping off his boot and sword. Like Erik, Marcus refused to wear a helmet. His hair lay matted against his skull, his locks fighting against the sweat to curl unruly again. A dried cut and bruise were forming near his right eye.

"There's no need to hold rank. The English are fleeing as fast as the fog that disappeared," Marcus called down.

Erik gave a single nod, sweeping the field with a quick glance. "I know. I don't want my men killing for pleasure. We've taken the land and river. It's the main water supply for the nearby towns. Our, Halfdan's goal, has been attained."

"Let the men get the kill out of their system. They're enjoying themselves."

Erik grabbed the horse reins from Marcus. He knew the horse would be startled from the venom in his voice more than the screams of horror rising from the field. "This is NOT your battle. Hold your tongue, or I'll cut it out for you and place it in your hand."

Marcus opened his mouth but swiftly closed it. Erik watched him run his tongue over his teeth as he wavered on the alarmed horse. Erik spoke quietly to the animal until its ears no longer flicked back and its hooves stopped dancing.

"I'll tell the men to hold their ground." Marcus pulled the reins from Erik's grasp and hurried off.

Scowling, Erik watched him ride off and glanced at the soldiers around him. None looked directly at him, but they were no longer killing. *Just looting off the dead – theirs and ours.*

Finally sheathing his sword but keeping his hand on its hilt, he walked back through his men. He wanted his horse, who still rested at camp, and needed to report to Halfdan. The tents would now need to be moved forward. He needed to find infantry men and select soldiers to stay back to help while others went off to the towns within the radius they had just attained.

He stepped over several dead Englishmen and said a small prayer for each. These men were not soldiers, but farmers and villagers. These men were unprepared to do battle. They attacked with pitchforks, short swords and other weak weapons. Their archers had been boys, too young to fight, let alone die. He sighed, half of him not wanting to be there and the other half reminding him of his duty and his father's legacy.

The battle – or fight – it seemed more of a fitting word, had been finished in three hours. Oddly, even after the late start, the sun stood in the sky, slowly making its way toward the west. Shortly after the archers stepped forward, the fog had cleared so quickly the enemy had no time to react. The dissipated fog showed the small count of English against their vast army.

It had felt satirical when the sun poked through and cleared the skies of grey. Some of the men had said it was an omen, a sign that this battle was blessed. Erik had kept his opinion quiet, thinking that it was a sign for the Saxons to open their eyes.

No longer walking through bloody mud, his boots made little noise as they stepped across the trampled grass. He reached camp and sent a few men with instructions toward the front lines. He then called the page boy to gather his horse. No one else would approach him unless necessary. They never did after battle. He debated about entering his tent to wash his hands but decided against, knowing Halfdan would turn the action into a snide comment of some sort.

Mounting his mare when the page returned, he kicked her into a full gallop in the direction of Halfdan's tents. The sooner he spoke with him, the sooner he could gather his troops and let them know Halfdan's order regarding the women. He needed to get back to the front lines before many of them left. He didn't want to have to travel into the towns to give personal warning.

Halfdan stood outside his tents, talking to an elder that had once been Erik's father's advisor. The older man gave him a warm smile and clasped both hands on Erik's shoulders once he'd dismounted.

"Well done, Jorgen's son! You look like your father returning, and 'tis a welcoming sight." The elder's voice came out scratchy but still strong.

"Thank you, my lord." Erik rested his hands on the man's forearms but said no more. The look of disdain on Halfdan's face prevented him from addressing the man by his name or showing the affection he would have preferred to give. He straightened and turned to Halfdan, making a conscious effort to erase all emotion from his face. "The battle was quick and satisfactory. The English were not prepared to fight men of our caliber."

"Yes, I've already heard the reports. Do you have anything else to add?" Halfdan's voice grated with irritation.

"No. You asked me to personally let you know the result." He would have added a few other thoughts but knew better.

"You will address me as Sire," Halfdan reminded him.

Again, Erik bit a sharp remark back, knowing full well he had authority of Halfdan. It might not be military, however it represented more than that. "I'd like to return to the men to inform them of your orders."

"Orders?" the elder asked, still standing beside Erik.

Halfdan spoke before Erik could open his mouth to respond. "I will not have our men fornicating with the women of this country. Our Saxon blood will not be watered down by this inferior race." His chest seemed to expand as he stared at the elder.

"I will have my leave then... if it's alright." Erik turned, not waiting for Halfdan's response or the elder's reaction to Halfdan's words. He swung onto his horse and headed back the way he had come.

It took less time than he wanted to reach the front lines. The battle finished, men cleaned their swords and weapons as the setting sun turned the sky a shade of pink. A few small fires burned in front of the field. Those in charge of clearing the dead worked out in the field behind the men. The English could gather theirs tomorrow in the daylight.

Erik spotted Marcus with another commander, Johan, near a fire, burning the blood off their swords. Their heads came up as Erik approached on horse. Letting his feet hit the soft earth, he reminded the men of the order. He tied his mare up near their horses and headed toward the next fire to speak to his men.

The reactions were as he had expected. The first group grumbled but knew better than to argue with him. The second lot included an enormous, burly Saxon wearing a necklace of human ears. Erik spoke Halfdan's order, his hand resting comfortably on his axe.

"Like hell," the rogue yelled. "I've earned my right to a few tarts followed by a slag and a slapper or two." The idiot had actually jumped up and now stood inches away from Erik, challenging him.

Erik stood his ground, ignoring the stench coming from the rotting ears, or possibly from the man himself. "You will not touch a woman or child. That is the order."

The giant laughed, hot breath splashing down on Erik's face. "I have the right to the spoils of war. 'Tis my right."

"Find yourself a pale of ale. Halfdan's word were clear: Our Saxon blood will not be watered down. You sire a child here and Halfdan himself will send an army after you."

The man took a step back and looked at the others in the circle, a cruel smirk on his face. "Fine, I'll find a woman and kill her when I'm finished. I'll even keep you happy, Master Jorgen, and kill her quickly with my knife. No teasing or torture." Spittle came from his mouth as he pronounced his t's, some landing on Erik's face.

Before the man had time to let his laugh erupt from his lips, Erik had his axe in one hand, the man's groin in his other. Gasps came from the circle but the giant said nothing, nor did he move a hair.

"Is it better I castrate you now? Prevent the wrong head from leading your thoughts?" Erik's voice split sharper than his axe. He'd not hesitate to remove the giant's manhood. If it would protect the innocent, he had no qualms about his actions.

The giant's Adam's apple bobbed up and down, however he said nothing.

"Answer me, soldier." Erik squeezed the man's bits tighter for emphasis.

"P-p-p-please d-d-don't." His voice now barely louder than a whisper.

"Not so fearless now, when your life mates are in my hands, are you? As I said, keep your bits in your pants." He gave a hard squeeze once more, putting the man out of action for probably the next week. He looked around at the men gathered around them. "This goes for all of you. Don't disappoint me."

Most of the men nodded or murmured in agreement. Erik knew the veterans would follow without question and they'd keep an eye on the new ones. He had no need to threaten them with spies watching and reporting back to him. His men would follow orders and most of Halfdan's would too. The crying giant now lying on the ground was example enough tonight.

He stepped over the man and toward the fire, warming his hands in the dancing flame. "Good job today, men. You fought like Saxons. Be proud of the land you've taken for our King in Denmark. Enjoy the spoils of the towns surrounding."

He glanced once more at the giant still lying on the ground and went back to the man. He leaned down and whispered in the man's ear, "Don't ever stand against me again. Next time I'll kill you before the words have finished rolling off your tongue." He stepped over the petrified man. Without looking back he gathered his horse, and he headed back to his tent to wash up.

Chapter 4

Linzi

The sun beat down on the field, sucking its moisture and making the soil impossible to break apart. It also burned through Linzi's scarf and heated her head. Her fiery hair acted as a sponge to the sun's rays. She used the back of her hand to wipe her forehead, and stood to stretch out her tired back muscles. She had been digging in the dirt and planting vegetables since sunrise.

Shielding her eyes, she looked up at the sun's position and realized it was well after lunch. Spring had come early this year, but it felt like summer poking its head out today. It must have known she had a lot of work to do outside and was laughing as she struggled to get it done.

She glanced at the row across from hers and saw Kenton about a hundred yards back, starting to catch up to her. His strength allowed him to dig quicker and deeper, but his hands were clumsy when it came to dropping the seeds and spreading the dirt. Her father had tilled the field yesterday with the horse, but because of the heat, it felt like it had been done a week ago.

She sighed and checked to see how much of her row remained unfinished. Another twenty minutes and it should be done. Then she'd go to the house to cut some bread and cheese for lunch. She needed to pour a large pitcher of water also. Just the thought of the cold, deep, well water made her swallow and remind her how thirsty she was. It didn't help that her tongue felt like it was caked in a layer of dirt as well. Bending over, she continued digging and planting, ignoring the moans of her body. Complaining wouldn't get the job done any faster.

"How 'bout I finish your row?" Her father's voice made her jump, only to wince a second later from the protest her tight leg muscles gave her. "You head back and make some food. I think your brother's going to pass out. He's been trying to get a drop from his empty canteen and keeps grumbling to himself that he'll fill it up when we eat," he laughed.

She did not argue with him. It meant faster time to the well. "I can't believe this heat. Of all days to have a cloudless day..." She let her words trail off as the sound of Kenton's voice stopped her. His canteen flew through the air past them.

Her father huffed quietly and warned the boy, "That temper is going to be the death of you, son."

"Mock the gods. Why is it so bloody hot?" He glared up at the bright sky. "Not yet summer and the air feels as if hell has come to earth."

Linzi turned and walked toward the small house, her brother and father moving their conversation away from the stifling heat and onto more appropriate reflections of hell on earth - the fighting in the south. She reached the top of the small hill near the house, cupping her hands over her face to see if she could visualize the edges of Northumbria, the northern tip of the large port city only a short distance from their farm. Why her father had vied for land on the southernmost tip of Scotland was still a mystery to her. Being near the eastern sea ports and enjoying the cool breeze off the ocean would have been her choice.

She dropped her hands and walked toward the house, her brother and father starting to make their way back as well. Cursing herself softly for tarrying too long, she rushed toward the small structure, knowing they would expect her to have prepared the midday meal already.

She slipped into the coverage of the modest home, her father having put all he was into keeping them well fed and taken care of, the man never uttering a complaint other than the occasional whisper of his longing for their mother. She walked to the cupboard and pulled the cheese from under a small cloth, the darkness of the closet giving the aging treat a place to keep cool. She walked toward the counter and worked to slice a few thick pieces off the larger chunk before working to carefully cut the bread without smashing it.

"I understand your desire to fight, Kenton, but you have to look at this from my point of view as well. Your sister cannot go without protection until she is wed." They walked in, Kenton moving toward her and slipping a piece of cheese from the cutting block before she could jab at him with a knife.

"If this is about me getting married, then please save the lecture. I will try to start going into town more often and hopefully by the birth of our Lord I will at least have a suitor or two." She shrugged, her father's gaze moving about her face.

"It will happen when it's supposed to happen. I'm just trying to explain to your brother that life is fleeting. We have no idea what tomorrow will bring and if something were to happen to me and your brother was away..."

Linzi reached out and touched her father's arm, squeezing softly. "I would make due, Da'. I know it's not proper to be forward as a lady, but I am strong and capable of most things. I agree that Kenton should remain with us, but if I am the cause of that..."

Kenton cut her off, bringing the conversation to a halt. "You're not. My lack of training is the issue. I haven't had a chance to go into town with the other lads as they start to prepare."

Linzi pointed to the small wooden table across the room. "Go sit and I'll bring the food to you."

The boys walked over and took a seat as she laid the bread and cheese before them. Three small mugs and a large pitcher of lukewarm well water and they were ready for the prayer. She looked at her brother and nodded, Kenton huffing loudly. His beef with the Lord was his own, but Linzi often wondered if he were just simply angry over their momma or if something else was eating at him.

"Bless us God and these gifts. Help tomorrow be better than today and wipe out the bloody Saxons."

Linzi rolled her eyes, her father's worn face lifting as he smiled. Their mother would never have approved of asking the Almighty to reach down and smite anyone, but the mood seemed to lighten at the very idea of killing the dastardly brutes off.

"Have you ever met a Saxon?" Linzi asked, reaching for the smallest piece of bread and cheese available. She tried to leave more food for her father and brother most nights. The boys had worked twice as much of the field as she had earlier.

"I haven't, but I've heard lots of stories." Kenton shrugged, shoving a large piece of bread in his mouth and trying to talk around it.

"Chew with your mouth closed," her father chided him before turning his attention to Linzi. "They are Vikings, a brute force of men from Denmark who care not for life or liberty. They have given in to the taste of victory, the elevation of feeling like a God. They are soulless creatures who cannot be trusted. We should all pray that somehow our brethren are able to defeat them in Midland, but if not, then for sure in Northumbria."

"What will they do with all of the land they've conquered?" Linzi asked, sitting back and holding her mug to her chest as if coddling it.

"They will rule it. They're killing off everyone as they move through the towns, the streets running with crimson rivers from the blood of the innocent."

She set her cup down and clasped her hands over her ears, not feeling so brave all of a sudden.

"Enough!" Her father yelled at her brother as Kenton's eyes diverted down to his lap.

"Sorry Da'." He reached over and tugged on Linzi's sleeve, a soft smile on his face. She dropped her hands, her heart racing at the idea of what the pilgrimage must look like.

"Your brother didn't mean to upset you. There is nothing for you to worry about. We will leave this place far before one of the depraved creatures shows up on our land." Her father slid closer to her, reaching out and pulling her against his side. He leaned over and kissed the top of her head. Linzi relaxed against him.

"They are trained to kill?" she asked quietly, her brother looking up at her as he reached for another piece of cheese.

"Much more than we are, but we will fight because this land belongs to us."

She sighed and closed her eyes, her thoughts dark as concern swept across her. "I know this is our land and I'd be prepared to fight too, but how do you defeat the devil?"

"With the light of truth and the hope that God will shine down on us." Her father patted her shoulder and moved back to his spot, reaching for more to eat.

Linzi took one last piece of bread and stood up. "I'd like to be excused for a bit. Just want to visit mother." She was referring to her mother's tomb, and knew her father would not argue.

He looked around her, trying to avoid making eye contact. "Of course. We'll meet down at the base of the hill shortly, just look for us."

She started for the door before pausing, turning to look over her shoulder. "How will I know if I ever run into a Saxon?"

"They are vicious men, their eyes full of hate and their words harsh. They would be quite dirty and wearing furs is a sure sign." Her brother looked up, his voice soft, but words spoken quickly as if they tasted sour.

"You'll never have to worry about that, Linzi. Ease your mind. The Saxons are far south and we will not let anyone get near you." Her father turned to wink at her before focusing back on her brother, their conversation picking back up about him joining the militia.

She slipped out into the noonday sun, the heat rolling over her in waves. Lunch had given her a much needed rest, but the afternoon would prove to be hard. They should have begun planting weeks before, the weather being so unpredictable in its willingness to be cold and then hot again from day to day. To plant their crops and have winter rear its head would be devastating. They were only able to survive from year to year because of the prior year's harvesting. Losing their seeds for any reason would leave them without.

She shuddered at the thought and pulled her scarf from her shoulders back over her head, the crimson strands of her hair dancing before her as the wind blew softly around her. She walked up to the top of the hill, sitting down next to her mother's grave and stretching her legs out.

The Saxons sounded like the stuff of nightmares, her visions of them comparable to the images of hell's demons that their pastors had warned of. She had no concerns about whether or not she would be able to tell a Viking from another man, now that her father and brother had warned her of what to keep watch for. The real question was whether the concern of seeing one was valid at all. The men in her life were protective, often overprotective, but one could never be too careful.

What would she do if one did happen upon their land, or if he cunningly closed in on her in town?

"I'd kill him without thinking twice about it." She reached over and rubbed the pollen from atop her mother's tombstone. "I'd ask for forgiveness from the Lord, but I would kill him, for surely if I didn't – he would not hesitate to slaughter me."

Chapter 5

Erik

Cold water splashed against his cheeks, his face downturned as he lost focus of the small pewter bowl before him, the liquid stained with the remnants of death. How long had he been fighting? How much longer might it last?

He stood, reaching for a cloth, as drops of water rushed down his chin and disappeared under his shirt, the smell of his own stench burning his nose. He wiped at his face before pulling his shirt from him and running the small cloth along his chest and arms. The countryside in Denmark swam before his vision, a smile touching the corners of his mouth.

He would covet the idea that one day after his duties were fulfilled and the war had ceased, that he would find a simple life, a place to dig in and grow roots. Nothing sounded more rewarding than seeing the end of strife and the return of peace among his father's people, but would that ever truly exist?

Where power beckoned the strongest of men to come and lay hold to its glory, there would always be greed and war. To conquer and take was a high like none other, and yet it stained him where he stood.

A long sigh left him as he finished washing up, his fingers brushing through his hair and scratching soft circles as he went. The men would be restless soon again.

He left his shirt sitting on a small wooden table within his tent, walking out with his small blade in his hand as he picked at the dried blood upon it and also cleaning under his nails. No matter how hard he tried, he never seemed able to cleanse it all away. He glanced up as some of the men grunted a welcome to him, the fire in the middle of the camp blazing rather largely. He looked around at the faces of his men, Marcus not to be seen.

Halfdan would most certainly not be found mingling with the common soldier. They might realize what a weak bastard he was if he spent too much time in the presence of true men of valor. Erik let his thoughts subside, his focus on the large flames that billowed before him. It felt almost too warm of an evening to sit before the fire and yet it offered a reminder that death wasn't the only principality of their time.

He moved to sit among the men, Johan seemingly in the middle of a thought. Everyone seemed to be paying attention to the younger commander, but he paused as Erik approached and took a seat beside him.

"Continue..." Erik spoke and Johan nodded, turning back toward the men gathered around them.

"I..." Johan paused, apparently unsure if he should continue his train of thought in front of Erik. He inhaled deeply and finished his words. "I pity the men from this country who had to send their sons to fight us today. The majority of those soldiers were nothing more than farmhands."

Not a sound came from around the fire except the crackle of wood. Erik watched the men to see if any would argue Johan's opinion. They expected him to remark as Halfdan would, but most who knew Erik, knew he would not. "T'is a pity to send boys in the place of men." He kept his statement simple and open-ended so no man or spy could report back to Halfdan.

"I saw several boys no older than me youngest son," a burley white-haired man spoke up.

"Their weapons were no weapons at all," someone else called out.

Erik knew these men had not gone into the nearby towns to ransack them. "And yet we choose not who we fight. We have a responsibility to follow the command of our King and leaders. If we were called upon to commit our own sons at the early age of seven, or eight, to fight for Denmark, then we would, would we not?" Erik pressed his forearms on his knees and looked around the crowd.

"Aye!" they all yelled in various timbres. His men couldn't spend too much time dwelling on the innocence of the enemy or their hearts would soften under their shirts and it would become a daunting task to take the next life, the boy at the end of their swords not old enough to have a family of his own yet.

"What of the women, Erik?" Johan asked, his voice steady and innocently questioning.

"Halfdan has a point in what he is requesting of us." He picked up a small stick beneath his foot and tossed it into the fire. "We are the great and mighty Celts. We cannot bastardize our great heritage by dimming the strong genes of our forefathers. We are as close to gods on earth as one might get. If we taint that with our sons, the next generation of our strength, then do we not weaken ourselves?"

"You're right, though my loins quite disagree." Johan laughed and Erik chuckled, knowing the feeling burning in his own body for pleasure. He stood and stretched before looking at some of his closest companions, most he would consider friends.

"Keep your noses clean and follow the orders given you. I don't want to cut any of you down, but I will do whatever necessary to maintain order and bring success to my father's name."

They all bowed their heads, their fists slapping against the breastplate of their chest as they muttered their agreement.

Erik made his leave, walking languidly toward the forest as he slipped his knife back in its place. He wanted a few moments to himself and hoped like hell that everyone else stayed put. The battle in front of them at Northumbria would not be as easy as the one they'd encountered at Midland.

England and Scotland had been at one another's throats over rights to the large landmass. A country divided against itself. To add in a claim from the Celts would call for the two countries to possibly lay down their arms against one another and join forces to press against Denmark. The very idea of a worthy battle caused his heart to palpitate, but his hate for death and waste quickly suffocated the excitement.

He knew there were other ways to feel passion, and war was just seemingly the one of choice.

Erik moved around the edge of the field before him, the trees offering very little coverage. He should be in his tent resting, but he longed to explore the small city beyond their camp. Death had come for all men who stepped up against the great Celt's that day. Several had lifted their hands in surrender and the men had flayed them regardless. He had to demand that they hold the line simply to teach them to be men and not transform into the demons the rest of the world believed them to be. It bothered him that some of the men enjoyed the command more than one should, and then coveted the belongings of the men as they bled to certain death. At times he felt he was a prince among the thieves.

With his hand on the hilt of his sword, he walked through the small town of Midland, the city dark and quiet, the lack of activity haunting him. He wore only his breeches and shoes, his chest bare. He stopped by a small wooden home, a candle in the window giving him a clue that life laid beyond the walls. He stood erect as the door cracked open, the soft cry of a female lifting into the air before the door slammed shut.

He wanted something to eat. Most homes in the wealthier parts of England and Scotland would have various amenities that he'd not been afforded for months. Being raised in his father's castle left him almost spoiled for comfort and yet he'd give it all up for a moment of peace. He put his shoulder against the door and pushed once with force. The door swung open, the woman on the other side screaming.

He shut the door and held up his hands, his face relaxing as to give the girl a bit of understanding.

"I am not here to harm you. I have given strict orders to not harm the women and children." He kept his hands up as the female backed up, a small boy sticking his head out from an opening just beyond the kitchen.

"Get back in the bedroom, Aldo." The small-framed woman motioned toward the boy and turned back to Erik when he disappeared. "What do you want? Have you not taken enough already?" Tears filled her eyes and spilled over onto her cheeks, the tracks of earlier tears giving way for them to drip down her throat. She pointed at his naked muscular chest. "You'll have to kill me if you think I'll let you touch me."

He breathed in softly and shook his head, making sure to take an obvious step back. "I need something to eat and drink and possibly a bath. After that I will be on my way."

"And the next demon who enters my home? Will he too only want food and me to draw him a bath? Or will he slit my throat as he did my beloved?"

The girl couldn't have been more than a year older than Erik, her dark hair pulled up in a messy bun, her white apron covered in the efforts of her work life. He kept his eyes on hers, wanting so badly to take in the rest of her figure, giving him something to envision in the shower while he relieved himself. He stifled a growl as desire pulsed through him, reminding himself quickly that he was a man and not a monster. He would never take a woman who did not want him. Never.

"No one else will bother you." He let his hands drop by his side. "I will make sure of it. Fix me something to eat and show me to the bath, and then you and the bairn can get back to your lives."

"What lives? You've taken everything from us." Her lips began to tremble, the hatred on her features clearly evident.

Her reaction did not surprise him. They were expected to hate him – he had taken everything from them, including their land. The future would prove to be harder than the moments that day. Death and war were a part of life that was to be expected. It was the loss of freedom, the subjugation that would clamp down their dreams and stifle hope. He locked his jaw as his thoughts ran him ragged.

"Fine," she barked out, turning to walk down a small hall. "There is a shower in the outhouse just beyond the back steps."

He moved behind her, his eyes trailing down the long slope of her spine, her thin dress giving way to soft curves that beckoned him to touch, to hold. Squeezing his hands into tight fists, he slowed his gait, letting her move a distance ahead of him. She opened the back door and reached up, grabbing a towel and bar of soap.

He took them from her and turned as she started to close the back door. "Do not lock me out. I'd rather not break your door, but I have no issue with doing so should you think it wise to deny me entry."

She said nothing as she closed the door. In the darkness the sounds of the night rushed to greet him. Still in nothing more than his breeches and shoes, Eye growing accustomed to the dark, Erik walked to the small outhouse. The crescent of moonlight giving way and creating something otherworldly. He looked up and laid a wish upon the great ball of light, his only desire for peace and love. He'd never share that with another, but in his own thoughts it was a reoccurring conversation.

A cleansing shower and relief to his loins made his mood lighten. He washed his breeches and still damp, redressed in them, oblivious to the cool night air. He walked back to the house, gently pushing the door and was partially relieved the woman had not locked it.

He sat down at the small table in the woman's quaint kitchen. She worked to warm meat and potatoes, her eyes adverted to him as he simply sat, staring into nothingness as she moved about him. Erik glanced down at the tugging of something on his pant leg, the small boy, no more than two years of age, smiling up at him.

The woman rushed toward the boy and scooped him away from Erik.

"I would not hurt the bairn."

She huffed. "You killed his father earlier today, and his young uncle. I would imagine you are capable of greater atrocity." She left the room, taking the boy with her as he clamored, trying to get back to Erik.

She returned a moment later, the cry of the small boy coming from a room beyond the kitchen. Erik left the conversation unfilled with his lack of response, his stomach aching for something warm and fulfilling. He ate quickly, the meal burning his tongue, but filling him to satisfaction. He stood, taking the loaf of bread with him. "Thank you."

Without further comment he turned to leave. He slipped out into the night, his emotions all over the place. He straightened and firmly locked them away.

He had no choice in the matter.

He was simply who he was born to be – a soldier.

Chapter 6

Linzi

The afternoon had been harsh, but evening brought sweet relief as Linzi prepared and shared a quick meal with her father and brother. They were too weary to speak about war or the weather. The three of them ate in comfortable silence. Her father had taken a turn to clean up, letting her slip off to bathe and get to bed early.

Kenton had mentioned earlier in the day that his mates would be stopping by tomorrow to help move some of the farm equipment. She wanted to ensure she looked her best, especially if Luke might be coming, though she didn't dare ask.

Very few men had blonde hair in their country; red or dark brown being the genetic tunes sung. Something about hair the color of the sun caused her stomach to tighten, the innocence of that specific appearance just calling to her. A smile played on her lips as her body responded to her thoughts of laying in the fields atop the hill and running her fingers through Luke's short hair, kissing his full lips. Her brother would kill them both if he knew she had begun to think of his mate in such a manner.

Luke would most likely pee his breeches if he knew Linzi had considered him for betrothal. She laughed at the thought, turning on her side and wishing the darkness of night offer her reprieve.

Morning came far too quickly, her father waking her to come and make breakfast with him. They had only a few eggs remaining, but the cheese and bread from the day before would have to suffice. Her father kept pushing her to hurry, their remaining items not enough to feed all of Kenton's mates. They would need to eat and have everything cleaned up by the time the boys returned from the nearby town as to not appear rude.

Linzi finished scrambling the eggs and sat down with her father, her brother nowhere to be found. "Has Kenton gone to town?"

"Yes." Her father seemed oddly quiet this morning. "I fear we'll have another fight on our hands when he returns."

"What have you done now?" Linzi picked up a small piece of bread, pinching a bit of egg between it and eating it slowly, savoring the richness of the meal. There was nothing better than eggs for breakfast and yet their two chickens couldn't produce nearly enough to allow them to have the treat more than once a week.

"T'is not I, this time. Jacob and Luke have joined the battalion going to Northumbria. They leave this afternoon. I fear your brother will once again be convinced of his duty to be beside them."

"He already believes that, Da'. Just remind him that his place is here." She did not want her brother to go to war. Nor did she want Luke there either.

Her father sat back, picking up his mug and taking a long drink. He smiled at Linzi and reached over, tugging at a long strand of her copper hair. "You're so beautiful – just like your precious mother was."

Sadness swept across the room, the loss of her mother never far from any of their thoughts. She had been a soft, gentle spirit, a comfort to them all. Linzi reached for her mug, bringing it to her lips and pausing as the sound of her mother's voice rushed through her thoughts, the woman everything Linzi hoped to be when she grew up. He was worried he would have to bury his son alongside his wife. A father should never outlive his son, or his wife. "You can talk sense into Kenton."

"I'm not sure it's worth it to try any more. He is of his own mind." The corners of his mouth turned downward. After a moment he forced them upward. "I fought in wars when I was Kenton's age; the fire in my blood for freedom and goodness almost overwhelming at times. It is time to let him part ways and live out his life as he sees fit. The farm will be left to both of you. Half for him should he ever choose to return and half for you and your future husband. The land is large enough to feed both your families. Your mother made me promise you have half. I swore I would see it done."

She reached across the table and rested her fingers on her father's arm, squeezing softly. She would most likely move when she married. However, no future betrothal would say no to the large amount of land that came with her as a dowry. "You know I will remain here with you until he returns."

The sound of male voices moving toward the house had her heart fluttering. Luke's laugh was contagious, his smile wide and goofy. He wasn't the most handsome of men, but something about him called to the girl in her that wanted to be in love. It did not stir the pressure of passion, even though she had yet to understand what that meant. Her mates had talked about it and she tended to keep her head down as they spoke. Without a mother to explain, she had no courage to ask what they meant. She was attracted to Luke's spirit, his demeanor, but lust wasn't a feeling that swam within her when he was near – that she understood.

Which left her with a feeling of comfort and serenity in its place. What need was there to feel the burning desire to behave like a heathen in front of a suitor? She never understood her mates' actions when they did that. The purpose of a woman was to find a suitable male partner who could produce strong offspring and support their family. Luke fit the protocol.

She straightened her back when her brother's fingers touched her shoulder softly as he moved to the table and started to pick at the remains of breakfast.

Her father flinched, but only she caught the subtle movement. "I can have Linzi make more if you boys are hungry?"

Kenton smirked and scooted toward Linzi as three boys moved into the small kitchen, squeezing into the table with them.

"No, we ate in town. Old Miss Larnz fed us bacon and eggs this morning."

"Then I am jealous." Linzi jabbed her brother in the ribs as everyone chuckled.

"Don't be. She's in need of company. She rattled off at the mouth the entire time we were there," Jacob spoke up, his mop of red hair sitting wildly on his head, freckles spread across his cheeks all the way to his ears.

"I would rather go hungry next time." Luke laughed and pointed to the boy sitting at the table who Linzi didn't recognize. "This is Peter. He joined the fight with us just this morning. He's from the North." Luke smiled at Linzi. "You look to have caught the sun."

She returned his smile. "Working the fields will do that. Kenton has the habit of disappearing and leaving it to me."

Kenton elbowed her in the ribs this time.

She introduced herself to Peter and when her father coughed she understood what he wanted. It was time for her to make herself unseen so lingering conversation about Kenton's plans could be worked out in the presence of the men.

She stood and nodded politely before slipping out of the room. She did not wait around to eavesdrop on the conversation. Instead, she grabbed her plaid wool shawl and clipped it together around her hips with her mother's Scottish thistle cape pin. She walked down to the field. In the cool morning air, she tugged the shawl from her hips and draped it over her head.

It wasn't half an hour later and she was covered in sweat, her shawl hanging on a nearby post, her arms shaking at the efforts of pushing the small shovel into the dirt. She would have to talk with her father about re-plowing the land. It was much too hard trying to plant. The elements hadn't allowed for any help in the matter. They needed rain and for once in her life, she couldn't believe she was praying for some. She stared at the grassy hill where a figure appeared. Luke walked down the hill, his hair catching the rays of the sun and almost appearing like it was ablaze.

"You're a hard working woman, are you not, Miss Linzi?" he commented when he stopped beside her, extending his hand for the small garden tool.

She handed it to him and sat back on her heels, her dress covering her legs down to her feet. She reached for her small canteen, taking a deep drink as the boy before her sunk to his knees and began pounding at the earth. "I know no other way." She smiled when he looked up and winked.

"My mother and sisters would be out here cursing up a storm."

"If it would bring a storm of rain, I would consider trying it." She laughed. "But your sisters would not. A lady does not curse."

He bent over and began stabbing at the ground again, the subtle muscles of his arms pressing through the thin cotton of his blue shirt. Butterflies swam in her stomach as she watched him, the first signs of courting being made apparent to her. Never before had any of Kenton's mates spoken directly to her without her brother being there. It wasn't the way. Someone might mistake advancement for mere conversation.

"You're right. A lady does not curse, but my mother has Irish blood in her and will tell you quickly that she is no lady. She would like you very much." He laughed, the light blue of his eyes reminding her of the water from the well just beyond their house.

"Then I would very much like to meet her one day." She frowned at herself as she realized her conversation was bordering on inappropriate. She quickly changed the subject. "Are you going to Northumbria?" Her frown faded as she offered him the water canteen, taking the shovel from him and idly picking at the ground once again herself.

"I am. This evening. I believe we need to protect what is ours and I cannot think of a better way to do it than giving up my hands and heart to serve this great country we've been blessed with."

I couldn't agree with you more. I would join you if I were allowed. She knew she could never say the words. Instead she said, "Be careful then. I should like to see you return." She smiled, heat rushing to her cheeks at the forwardness of her words.

"What are you two doing?"

Her brother's voice immediately stopped the conversation. Linzi's heart contracted hard in her chest at the sound of question upon her brother's tongue.

Kenton moved beside Luke as the blonde-haired boy stood and pressed his chest to Kenton's, her brother's face red, his expression angry. Luke appeared calm but ready to fight. "We were talking. A conversation about war for this land."

Kenton pushed Luke's chest, the two of them moving away from Linzi as they prepared to fight. She looked up the hill to see her father rushing toward them, his hand in the air, his voice commanding, "Enough!"

The boys paid no heed. Kenton shoved Luke again. This time Luke came back, arms swinging.

Linzi hurried to stop them, but quickly realized she would cause more harm – to them and herself. Her father would bring an end to the misunderstanding. She had no problem letting her brother feel like the arse he was.

"Stop it! *Stop it!*" Her father moved between them, turning to glare at his son. "What is the meaning of this?" Even though he was twice their age, he pulled the two boys apart as if they were children.

Kenton jabbed a finger at Luke. "He has no right to be out here talking to her!" He spat as he shouted the words out and tried to break free of his father's hold to hit his mate again.

"Your sister did not mind, nor did not ask me to leave." Luke wiped the blood running down his lip that Kenton's fist had connected with earlier.

Luke's teasing comment sent Kenton struggling to attack him again.

"Enough!" Linzi's father roared. "Did you not think a day would come when a suitor might offer your sister the life she deserves?"

Kenton looked over his father's shoulder, growling. "It will not be my damn mate. Especially this one."

Linzi stared wide-eyed at her brother. She wished the ground would swallow her up. Whatever inclination Luke had, probably just disappeared because of her stupid-arse brother.

"Why would you not want your sister, whom you love so much, to be taken care of by someone you trust?" Luke yelled back.

Linzi's stomach contracted tightly.

He *had* been courting her.

"Never!" Kenton stomped his foot. "I will not have my sister laying with someone... someone who..." He hesitated as he glared at Luke. "Someone I've spent my life with. Drank with, shared longings and stories with."

Linzi shook her head, not understanding what Kenton was ranting on about. "What does it matter?"

Kenton turned his death stare on her. "You have no idea."

"I will slit Luke from throat to groin should he hurt my mother's daughter," Kenton yelled again until their father pushed hard at the boy's chest.

"I said, stop it. While I am alive and you live here and under my roof, you'll heed my words."

Air forcefully expelled through Kenton's nostrils, but he did not argue with his father. "I'm only concerned for Linzi."

"Luke is a good man. He'd make a fine husband."

"For someone else's sister." Kenton shook his head. "He leaves with me tonight. What are the odds that either of us will return?"

Linzi released a soft sound of fear, her fingers coming up to press upon her lips. Kenton turned to her, a look of sorrow on his face that made her want to cry. She was her father's daughter so she would not. She would be strong, as strong as the highlanders in front of her.

It did not work. She couldn't stop the wetness from escaping her eyes. She rushed by them, running back toward the house. She had promised her father she would support whatever decision Kenton made in joining the army, but she hadn't expected him to actually join. She raced up the hill, past her mother's marker stone which only made the reality of losing someone she loved all too real.

Of course, Kenton was right.

He and Luke would die fighting the demons from Denmark. The stories of their skill and treachery spread far and wide. The land sat in silent terror at the great evil known as the Vikings. They moved through the countryside, laying waste to everything. The number of women and children killed by their swords was innumerable, their taste for carnage and death unsated.

She walked into the house, her lungs burning, eyes filled with hot tears. She looked out the door to see her father berating her brother, his mates standing nearby with solemn looks on their own faces. Did they not know what they were walking into? Did they not care?

She stared out the window to the hill where her mother rests, the small tomb standing out against the green grass and large tree beyond it. She would be burying Kenton beside their beloved matriarch, her brother now a dead man walking. Tears again spilled over onto her cheeks as a soft sob left her lips.

Why would God allow such a thing to wash over them? Why?

Chapter 7

Erik

The morning sun filtered through the tent, Erik having laid awake all night planning for the battle that would occur later in the lunch. The men needed to rest after the short squirmish yesterday and, by midday, the group Halfdan had selected would march to the eastern seaboard and take the city with a frontal attack. Of course he would select Erik's men to fight. He always did.

There would be an impressive fight presented to them there. Erik believed they needed all the men but Halfdan refused him. Erik had argued that most of Northumbria was made up of sea-faring men who were strong. They were trained to deal with pirates. The ships would be of no concern against the fleet they had. The English ships were built for trade, not battle. However, the weapons might be a little more refined than pitchforks and kitchen knives. Halfdan had mocked him and called him a coward.

Annoyed, Erik sat up, running his hands through his short blonde hair before quickly dressing and stepping out into the early morning fog. He walked toward the small fire where a few of his commanders huddled. He spoke quietly, "Gather the men and let us make haste. It's time to push forward and take Northumbria today. It'll be a battle worthy of our training. Let our families speak that over the other battles. Tell your men and incite in them a desire to prove themselves in this fight. We'll need our hearts on fire and our concentration tunneled."

He turned as they loudly resounded his commands. Marcus walked toward him and handed him a small mug of steamy beverage. He reached for it and took a long drink, the bitterness of the coffee bringing him into awareness. Marcus had cut his hair off – all of it.

"What did you do to yourself?" Erik smirked and reached to rub his cousin's bald head.

Marcus jerked out of the way with a scowl on his face. "Lice has broken out among the men. I refuse to be the host to any parasite. Disgusting fucking country." His face contorted as he turned and nodded toward the large tent that sat at the northern end of their camp. "King Halfdan wants to see you."

He's not my king, or yours. "When did you become his messenger?"

Marcus ignored him and stood defiant.

Erik would not be easily disregarded. "The order was given to me this morning to see him, and yet you come to tell me again?" He moved toward the tent, looking over his shoulder at Marcus with warning. He stomped back, his chest inches from Marcus'. "If you want my position then come and take it. I dare you. I'll not so easily give it up."

Nothing would piss off his angst-filled cousin more than being put in his place. Naught would incite rage in him like Erik talking down to him. It wasn't something Erik reveled in, but a taint sat upon Marcus, a darkness that left Erik on guard at times. The boy acted bitter that his future did not hold a crown. Marcus' life would always be coated in fighting and foreign travels.

Erik's father, Jorgen, had two sons. Erik was the younger of the two, his brother Nathaniel now sat on the throne in Denmark after his father's death. Erik was a prince, second in line to the throne until Nathaniel's son was born. Erik never asked for his position but he understood duty over everything else. His father had instilled that in his sons the moment they could walk.

Nathaniel had yet to establish clarity of his own rule. His father had been controlling and manipulative – even from the grave. He had been a just king and the people loved him for it. He craved more land and more of everything for his kingdom.

His reign did not end with his death. The long list of final commands for the kingdom left Nathaniel to lay waste to his own desires and finish fulfilling his father's. Erik brushed his hand along his face, his thoughts shifting from his brother back to his cousin. They were all puppets – pawns in someone else's game.

He paused in front of Halfdan's tent, letting his fingers rub the outer material which held the elements at bay before moving in. He needed to talk with Nathaniel about his concerns, about the blasphemy of their commander in chief allowing others to label him as the King of the Celts. Nothing could be further from the truth, and if Halfdan thought Erik wouldn't speak up to correct the gross inaccuracy, he was wrong.

"Sire, you called?" Erik spoke loudly, pushing the tent opening aside, but waiting for the large brute inside to invite him in.

"Enter," Halfdan barked.

Erik stepped in, the small flame of a candle lighting up the large area. Halfdan's tent was easily the size of four regular tents, the bastard unwilling to share the space with anyone, which left them with a good-sized handful of men sleeping beneath the stars, or huddled together as men should never be, in the smaller tents. Hatred washed through him and he stifled it. Black emotions would only pull him down further, his own heart struggling to remain pure in the fields of blood that life in battle had presented.

"As we spoke yesterday, I will lead the men today into battle again."

Erik bit his tongue to hold back the mention that it was he who had led the men, not the coward of a man on the white horse.

"My victory yesterday was nothing more than a foreshadowing of the great success we will have today." The large man turned from a full length mirror and adjusted his vest. He frowned at Erik, his eyebrows pressing together in a hairy mess. "I do applaud you for containing your men and their wanton desires last night. However, I want to know what the hell you were doing in that heathen woman's house? Did you not think my commands apply to you as well? Do you believe you are above me?"

Erik crossed his arms over his waist, anger swimming in his chest. He didn't know what angered him more; Halfdan's accusation or the fact that he had been followed. "I ate and showered."

"And I am to believe you?"

Erik's feet twitched with the urge to lunge at his superior officer. "I would never take advantage of a woman. No matter your commands."

"Ahhh, so you say." The large general shook his head in disgust. He reached for his over-sized mug, taking a long drink and then licked at his mustache and scraggly beard. "And if I were to command you to take a woman and make her scream in pleasure in front of us all?"

"I would refuse," Erik responded, shrugging as if the conversation hadn't begun to burn his insides. By right, he should flay the large bastard before him. He was crude and unrefined – dark and evil, but he had been more than effective and Erik's father had grown up as friends with the bastard, his adoration for Halfdan the only reason the bastard held position still.

"Then I would kill you." Halfdan did not bat an eye as he said the words.

Something stirred inside him... a warning of some kind? "Then I suppose you would know how to relieve the country of their prince should the time come for you to enact your plans."

Halfdan laughed, the sound crude and thick. He walked over and slapped Erik on the shoulder, looking him in the eye as the sound died. "There may be some of your father in you yet." His face steeled. "My loyalty is the crown of Denmark. Just remember you are still under me. You were not the first male your mother birthed."

"I know where I stand." *Do you?* Again Erik bit the comment back from leaving his tongue. "What would you have of me today, Sire?" Erik stood stiff, his features proud and his eyes set on his commander. Their bantering would have to resurrect another day. The trip to Northumbria would take most of the morning and they were wasting it away with a pissing contest that would never move beyond the dank walls of the tent in which they stood.

"Tell your commanders to stay close to the eastern coast, the seas giving us coverage as we slip up the shoreline. I want you in the back with me. You are to cover me."

"Sire," Erik cut him off. "My position is with my men."

Halfdan gave his head a single shake, one similar to what Erik's father used to do. "You may ride your horse today, but our soldiers will do the killing. You are to instruct them of our goals and strategy before we attack, and then you are on protection duty. The people would fall to despair should anything befall me."

"I believe you have the ability to protect yourself." Erik knew the battle would not be easy. The fact that Halfdan wanted to hide like a frightened child angered him. It was not the Viking way.

"You are not in the position to argue with your duty." Halfdan glared at him. "Beside me. If I die, it will be after a sword has pierced your heart and your head has rolled apart from its body."

"You think you are the next King of England. It is new territory for Denmark as far as the people are concerned. It is not your land." Erik couldn't help himself, his chest lifting as he breathed in the rightness of his accusation.

Halfdan moved toward him, his large face square in front of Erik's. "I am not the people, and yet they find me more worthy than your simpleton brother to lead our great country." He stared at Erik, his face of mask of controlled rage. "Your father himself would have dethroned Nathaniel and put me in his place had he known how useless your brother is. Do not forget your place, Erik. You have no more right to the crown than I do, and if we make it through this fight for land you will find yourself bowing before me. The people will have their wish, so choose your side, *boy*."

Crimson filled his gaze as he stared at Halfdan, the longing to massacre the man before him washing over him in great waves. He steeled himself, his jaw locking into place as a tremor ran through him. He might never be king, but he would be damned if the bastard before him ever held the crown. He would commit treason and kill the man with his own bare hands. Maybe even take pleasure in that death for once. Today was not the day. Erik let his shoulders drop. "Protection duty today. Got it. I shall inform the men we'll be mobilizing in thirty minutes." Erik turned and slipped out of the tent, reaching for a pot of hot water that bubbled in a small cauldron and slinging it with all his might. It launched beyond the camp and was lost to the woods, but the burnt line across Erik's hand would be a reminder. He was human and not a monster. He would fight this fight and win more land for his father's cause, but he would never sink to the level of depravity Halfdan would.

He needed to keep a keen eye on the man, and with protection duty for the next battle, it would not be a problem. He would need to find someone he trusted to send word back to Denmark. The large waterway between the two lands would prove different to master with only one man. Spies and knowing who to trust seemed to be dwindling the longer they spent in this forsaken land. Tattle tailing would have to wait another day.

Erik moved to the center of the camp, cupping his hands over his mouth and yelling loudly through his blistering fingers, "You have half an hour to be ready to move out. Mobilize Great Army of Denmark. We will claim victory to the largest port city this side of Scotland and its people will come to bow before us. Mobilize and take what is rightfully yours, for you are gods of this earth and the world will know it today. ARISE VIKINGS!" He hollered with all his might, his voice deep and boisterous as cheers from the men wrapped around him, almost deafening.

The men filed in behind him as they began to travel, a small group of them remaining behind to clean the evidence that the great Vikings had ever stopped to rest. The more the world believed they were above the commonalities of man, the better. Marcus rode up next to Erik as the army moved in the silence of pre-battle. A few soft murmurs drifted across the men but, for the most part, weariness sat on all of them like a wet cloak along with the solemn thought of death others might succumb to.

"Where will you be in the battle today, commander?"

Erik looked toward his cousin, the other man as good as he was at hiding his disdain. He knew where Erik was to stand and his jealous, mocking tone gave clear evidence. Marcus was the son of his father's youngest brother, the most suited in his looks and attitude for a royal life and yet the furthest from ever tasting it. "I will be beside our captain, guarding him and his bright white stallion."

"That horse is no more attention-drawing than a man who stands above the others in height with his golden-white hair." He nodded toward Erik and smirked. "You should cut it all off and save yourself the realization the bugs have reached your own scalp."

"I find it quite hard to believe a man who would murder children and rape women would be so put off by small fleas that do nothing more than eat dirt from one's hair," Erik chuckled, the smirk leaving his cousin's face.

"It's unnatural."

"Pillaging and killing is unnatural. Bugs living on dirty surfaces and being what they were created to be is quite natural, cousin."

"Whatever. The tiny vermin disgusts me to no end." Marcus shrugged, reaching up to brush his hand over his bald scalp. "Did you lay with a woman last night? The men have been talking. They noticed you were gone for quite some time from the camp."

"I didn't touch anyone. I followed command. Simply found a place to shower and a warm meal to fill my belly." He turned his gaze back to the men in front of them, their shoulders pulling forward from over exertion. "There was a small boy in the house. He reminds me now why I'm doing this."

"How could a useless child remind you of war?"

"He reminded me of my own desire to finish this and go home. I'm ready to find a wife and have boys of my own." Erik glanced at Marcus, who simply scoffed.

"This is real living! Revel in this feeling, because no small crying babe, or tight cunt between the legs of a busty woman will provide nearly the level of ecstasy that can be found here. Power is the essence of pleasure."

Erik let Marcus' words sink in but did not respond. He disagreed on every possible level.

Chapter 8

Linzi

It took no time at all for Kenton to pack the few things he would need for the trip to Northumbria. Her brother pulled her into the yard while the other boys waited by the road. She stood before him, her long hair dancing about as if embodied with a life of its own. As the wind rose, Kenton batted a strand of her hair away from his face and reached out, taking her shoulders.

The day had been wasted on tears, the field as unworked as it was just after breakfast. She looked up at him, the perfect blend of her mother and father staring back at her. He was her blood, her only mate and yet the days of playing were long gone.

"You know I love you." He swallowed hard, his own eyes filling but no tears fell.

"Yes," she whispered, her brow creased and her heart aching painfully in her small chest. She reached out and pressed her hands around his ribcage, tears filling and flowing from her eyes yet again.

"I need to do this, Linzi. I need to go and protect what is rightfully ours. One day my family and yours will live on this lot. If the Vikings come and take it then we have nothing." He paused, reaching up to wipe a tear that rolled down her face. "You understand, right? I will not let anyone touch mother's stone."

"I am not fearful of your going, it is your return that leaves me doubting." She turned and looked at the hill where their mother lay, long gone from her grasp. She looked back at her brother as a cocky smile lifted his lips.

"I'll be here all the days of your life to drive you mad." He pulled her close, Linzi tucking her face into the softness of his chest and wrapping her arms around him. She squeezed him hard and let her eyes move toward the waiting men, Luke lifting his hand toward her.

She waved at him and looked back at her brother. "Don't kill Luke please. He's your only mate who's nearly handsome enough for me to want to roll in the sheets with."

The look on her brother's strong features caused her to laugh, a soft snort following, which edged Kenton to laugh too. He looked back over to the men, Luke turning and staring out at the large field surrounding them.

"Yeah, better look away, you shite."

Linzi swatted at her brother before pulling him in for one more hug. He would return and they would live out their days together, her family small but mighty in care and adoration for each other.

"I love you. Be careful."

He leaned down and kissed her forehead. "Should I not return," his voice choked with emotion, "I beg you to take sword to throat before one of those brutish Vikings can lay claim to you." He turned and hurried to the other boys.

Linzi gasped and nearly fell crumpled to the ground. It took everything just to concentrate on walking to the opening of the house where her father stood. She leaned against the door frame, her father coming to stand behind her as they watched her brother leave. Torrid emotions pulled at her resolve to be strong and she inhaled a shaky breath, her father's strong hands rubbing her shoulders.

"He will come back. I promise it." He leaned around her and kissed the side of her face before disappearing into the house.

She stood and watched until the boys were nothing more than pinpoints on the horizon, the sun high in the sky and the heat scorching. Her father could promise her nothing. He had promised her mother would not die when she fell ill. When it came to death, no deal with the devil could change his mind.

She finally walked into the house and screamed when her father fell to the bench beside the table, his face pale and unnaturally wet. She hurried over to him, reaching to touch his head before cursing softly.

"Da', you're running fever!" She rushed to the small cupboard and pulled out a fresh hand towel, dipping it in a small basin of water and wringing it out as she hurried back to her father. She wiped his face and tilted her head in order to look him in the eyes. They were bright, and not because of unshed tears. She had no idea how long he had been ill, the heart-wrenching decision of her brother had clouded her mind from noticing anything else.

"I'm good, child. Just a little off. Perhaps the eggs weren't as fresh as I thought." Concern covered his features as he had trouble focusing on her, his hand shaking slightly as he reached to touch her cheek.

"It's not the eggs. Let's get you in bed. Perhaps it's just a small bug due to the stress of everything." She reached down and helped her father stand, walking with him to his small cot. He sat down, a loud painful groan leaving his lips.

Linzi did not like how he didn't argue with her and how his pallor had gone to a deathly white color. She debated on running to get her brother, but knew her father would never allow her.

He lay curled in the bed, like a newborn. His tired appearance too sudden for her liking. She pushed his chest and beckoned him to lay onto his back. He obliged and moaned softly, his eyes closed as if in pain.

She removed his shoes and socks, rubbing his hand as she sat beside him on the small cot. "I'm going to the well to get cool water."

"Do not leave the property, Meredith."

Linzi blinked. Meredith was her mother's name. Was he becoming delirious? So quickly? It frightened her.

"Stay close to the house. It's just me and you now."

"I'll stay by the house, Da'. The seed planting can wait another day."

His breathing grew heavy. When Linzi thought he was asleep, he inhaled a sharp breath and spoke clearly, "Take care of yourself until this passes and then I shall be there to take care of thee."

She did not understand what he meant, but his breathing eased and she realized he had fallen asleep. She moved toward the head of the bed, picking up the cloth and bathing his forehead with the cool rag as she sang softly, the melody a song her mother often sang when she was ill with the fever. She waited until a deep snore of his rest gave her proof he was finally resting.

It was Wednesday, which meant that Martha, her best friend, would be coming to visit that afternoon. Their parents allowed them one afternoon off together and had for the longest time. She watched her father for a minute more and then retired to the kitchen, cleaning up and working to cut a few slices of minced meat her father had cured the day before. She cut a long strip of cheese and tore off a hunk of bread, plating everything and setting it on the table for her lunch with Martha.

Linzi picked up the small water jug and slipped it under her arm, walking out of the shadows and down the far western slope of the house to the well. Trees rest around the opening then sunk deep into the earth, the air easier to breathe right around the well's entrance. Linzi set her jug carefully on the ground beside her and reached up, unhooking the rope that held the small bucket suspended in the darkness below her. She maneuvered the bucket to dip into the water, the sounds her only proof that she was doing it right.

She moved back and wrapped the rope around her hands twice, leaning back and pulling with all her strength. The bucket was heavy and she wrestled with it to get it to the surface, careful in her approach to lift it from the top of the well. She found success, pouring the ice-cold water into the pitcher and tying the rope back in place.

Her father always made her brother draw the water, but today was the start of a new life, one where she would begin to learn how to do a whole list of things she never knew before. Sadness clung to her over Kenton leaving and yet it was adventuresome to consider the possibilities. Linzi walked back toward the house, the sight of her friend's plaid blue dress catching her attention.

"Martha! Up here!!" Linzi yelled and jogged toward her. Water splashing on the front of her dress forced her to stop. She cursed, "Shite!"

She wiped what water she could off, then cupped the jug to her chest between her breasts and walked carefully toward the approaching girl. Martha smiled and waved, her long brown hair twisted into braids. Linzi missed the hours her mother would spend doing the same to her. Her poor father did not have the coordination when she was younger and most days she left it free. She'd given up on having her hair done long ago, but often found that Martha would ask to do it on Wednesday and for that day alone she could feel pretty, perfectly feminine.

"You want me to help?" her friend asked, reaching for the jug.

Linzi handed it to her and walked closely by her friend, looking down. She tried to shake the wetness against her breasts. The water had spilled there too.

"The water's freezing. You might want to change when we get back."

"Naw... I've outgrown most of my clothes again, so this is one of the two dresses I still have. I'll save the other for tomorrow seeing that I hate washing the laundry."

"Me, too. I have three younger sisters and for some reason momma always calls me to do the washing. I think she secretly hates me." They laughed and Linzi turned as they reached the door to her small house, putting her finger to her lips.

"Da's got a fever, so let's keep it down."

"We can just go up on the hill if you want?"

"Let's eat the lunch I made us and then we can go up there to talk. Mother likes to hear our conversations anyway."

Martha smirked and rolled her eyes, walking in and setting the jug down as Linzi grabbed two small mugs and slipped her legs into the wooden bench of the table, patting beside her.

"Sit and tell me of life in the big city."

Martha reached behind her, taking the string of her dress in her neck and tugging, the top coming loose. "First, let me show you something, but you have to promise not to tell anyone. No one knows."

"I wouldn't tell a soul, besides, you're my best friend." Tightness pulled at Linzi's chest, her eyes wide with wonder as she tried to imagine what Martha had done. She was unruly and often got in trouble, but being one of twelve kids, Martha had to do *something* to garner attention.

She dropped her dress just above her chest, a lovely red rose sitting on the soft skin just above her left breast. Linzi clamped her hands over her mouth and yelped softly, Martha laughing and pulling her dress back on. She reached to tie it and growled, moving to stand with her back to Linzi.

"Tie this for me."

"You got a marking on your skin?"

"Yes, and you should too. It makes you feel free."

"Free? I thought they used needles to drill that dye into your flesh."

"Well, they do, but it's not as bad as you think."

"Who did it?"

Martha moved from Linzi and sat down, reaching to grab a piece of cheese as Linzi swatted at her. "Let's pray over the food and then you'll tell me all about it."

Martha nodded and said a quick prayer for them before shoving a piece of cheese in her mouth, her hazel eyes filled with mischief.

"I actually did it."

"I know you did it. I just saw it. I want to know how badly it hurtcha."

"No," Martha whispered, shaking her head, "I mean I drew the rose on my own chest."

"What? How? It's upside down for you." Linzi sat back, her lip turning up at the thought of stabbing her own self with a needle.

"I've been drawing for years, you know that. I just didn't tell you that I had figured out how to do this. They call them ta'ttoos."

"That's because they are taboo." Linzi shook her head. "What's your husband going to think of that on your wedding night?"

"Wedding night? Bahhh. I'm laying with a man long before my wedding night."

"That is not true and you know it. Your mother would kill you."

"She doesn't need to know. Now... you want one?"

"A man before I'm married? I'll wait." Linzi knew she was stalling and Martha saw right through her.

"A tattoo. I'll give you one."

Linzi took a small bite of the bread in front of her, her eyes narrowing at her friend. Did she want someone stabbing at the soft flesh of her chest with a needle? No. Did she want to expose herself to ridicule and possibly being called a harlot? No. Did she want this freedom Martha talked about? "I'm scared it'll hurt."

"Well, I brought some of my Da's stout. You drink it and then I'll make you a bed of roses on your shoulder." Martha wagged her eyebrows, patting the small brown bag that sat beside her, the strap still hanging on her shoulder.

"Why my shoulder?"

"Because it's sexy. We'll line your shoulder with roses and you can imagine your beau kissing his way around them. And I have one on my breast. That was my idea and I don't want anyone else to have one there."

Heat rushed to Linzi's cheeks and throat, the idea of a man kissing her anywhere stealing her breath and elevating her pulse. She knew her father would expect her to be a complete lady until the time of her wedding and the Lord would demand it. Good thing Luke was homely and not a real looker, otherwise she'd have to fight against the lust that some of the more adventurous girls made reference to.

"Where are we doing this?"

Martha shoved a piece of meat in her mouth and got up, walking toward the door and peering out. "Let's go up there on the hill and do it. We need to get moving though. It's going to take a while."

"How do you know it's going to turn out okay? I don't want to stain my skin and then it looks horrible."

Martha walked back to the table, pulling a small piece of paper from her bag and handing it to Linzi. The most beautiful array of pink roses ran across the page and Linzi knew without a doubt that they would make her feel beautiful. She might not have her hair done as often as the other girls, but decorated in the most beautiful flower known to man, she would be radiant.

"Let me check on father and then we'll go. You have all the stuff you need?" She couldn't believe she was doing this.

Martha nodded and picked up her bag, reaching to grab one more piece of cheese before moving out of the house again.

Linzi rubbed her father's head softly, the fever seeming to have broken just enough for him to be comfortable and her to be less than terrified. She would need to go into town the next day and get him some herbs if she could find someone willing to trade.

She left him and joined her friend, the two girls walking up the steep hill beside the house, chattering about boys and dreaming of falling deeply in love. Linzi slipped the top of her dress off her shoulders, tucking the material under her armpits and sitting down in front of Martha. She took a long sip of the liquor, a sound of disgust leaving her. "That's the vilest stuff I've ever tasted."

"I know, right? I hate it too, but it's good for forgetting, and numbing your nerves if you have to do something like this or have sex with a boy."

"Have sex with a boy?" Linzi looked over her shoulder. "Who told you that?"

"My momma did." She laughed and leaned in, patting Linzi's shoulder with her other hand. "This is going to sting, but just keep drinking and you'll be right as rain soon."

"Okay," Linzi muttered, her eyes moving toward the small house that hovered above her all her life. She wanted to drown out the pain of her brother leaving, the responsibility of her ill father, the ache of her mother not being here. She yelped at the touch of the first needle and lifted the drink to her lips, taking in a few gulps and spitting. Her father would die if he saw her, her brother would kick her arse and most likely, Momma was rolling over in her grave.

Chapter 9

Erik

The clan of men approached Northumbria just before the noon-day sun hit the highest point in the sky, the fog long dissipated due to the sun's rays. The English littered the tree line just inland, two of Erik's scouts confirmed the news when they both returned. There were more English than they had expected, but the energy dancing across the Celts around him spoke of victory no matter what. Some of them would die today, but for King and Country and, of course, for the glorious Viking death in battle – what better way to go? He moved toward the front, turning to speak to the men.

Halfdan moved in front of him, his large white horse perfectly clean and brushed.

Erik tugged on the reins of his animal, moving her back a few steps as to not be so close to the leader. He had yet to enter a battle that he hadn't given the speech before, but things were changing. The large oaf in front of him was getting desperate. Erik let his thoughts dissipate, Halfdan's ability to fight almost spawned from birth, though ironically he never fought much. Erik wondered if the man had ever been in the heart of a battle. He believed Halfdan had killed many men, he just couldn't grasp it was done the proud Viking way.

Erik too had been taught to wield his sword or axe ever since he was a child. The weapons now mere extensions of his arms. The thought ushered in disappointed relief, the odd sensations tearing at the various parts of his soul. He remembered the small boy in the house the night before, the protective, defiant young woman rushing to save him from threat.

A smile touched his mouth at the thought of taking the boy in his lap, the woman leaning over and kissing him with loving passion before ruffling the boy's hair. Now that was ironic. How badly he wanted a different existence. He wished he could sever himself in two, one part of him chase after his plain life, the other hold the grandeur of a Viking strong in battle.

The sound of his commander's voice brought him back to the present. "Isn't that right, Erik?"

"What's that, Sire?" He wondered if his men listened to him the same way he had ignored Halfdan. He hoped not.

"Were you not paying attention to *my* commands?"

He was being tested, and most likely used to be made an example of. "I was busy killing the bloody English in my head, Sire."

The crowd of men laughed, a battle cry rising up as their true leader spoke of death and carnage. Erik sat up straight, his eyes filled with challenge as he waited for the reprimanding that was sure to come. Or Halfdan was baiting him. The man could not be trusted.

"Let us move forward then. As requested, you will ride beside me. Do you have anything to add today?"

He did not miss the hush that spread through his men at Halfdan's comment. He had turned his command to stay at his side into something Erik had requested. He moved up beside Halfdan, a wicked smile on his lips, all thoughts of love and desire falling cold. As he turned his horse, Halfdan's white mare to shuffle in fear. Erik cleared his throat. "It is time to take and plunder. If we are not good at anything else, we are damn good at this!" Right or wrong, it was in their Viking blood. "Let us take what is already rightfully ours! Who's with me?"

The crowd went wild, axes and swords littering the air as the men threw their hands up, chanting and pumping their weapons as a show of support.

Erik looked over at a scowling Halfdan. "By your command, Sire."

"For Denmark!" Halfdan shouted.

"And our great King!" Erik roared, knowing full well Halfdan would never say those words.

The men cried out as they rushed the large open field, the English marching in a formation that wouldn't hold for more than a few moments. A Scottish flag flew in the back of the group. Erik realized then that the additional troops weren't English, but a response to help from their neighbors. The Scots had finally joined the fight.

"They called for backup." He looked over at Halfdan and nodded toward the Scottish flag. The match appeared evenly paired man to man, but the skill of the Celts far outweighed that of the men before them. Erik usurped three attempts on Halfdan's life in the first few minutes, the older man not giving credit for any of it.

As the battle raged and arrows flew in every direction, the men were losing rank in the front. They needed him there. "I need to join the front lines. Have Marcus defend you and I'll go."

"No!" Halfdan nearly hid behind Erik, cowering. "Send Marcus to the front. You remain with me."

"I'm here to kill the English and take the land for us, remember?"

"For me."

"What?"

"Take the land for me." Halfdan pounded his chest. "Send what's left of your infantry in."

"You want to kill my men?" Erik asked incredulously.

Halfdan choked out, "They are MY men! I can do whatever I want with them!"

"This is madness!" Erik wanted to knock the man unconscious. "You serve the crown as I do," Erik barked out, his heart pounding in his chest as his remaining men rushed to help the others. They too began to fall on the front lines of the attack.

"And you serve me!" Halfdan hissed.

That was the last straw. Erik pressed his lips tight and then shook the reins. His horse shot off toward the front lines. He slowed only when he came beside Marcus. "Go back and protect Halfdan with your life. He is in need of babysitting."

Marcus put his sword through a man's chest and scowled at Erik. "What the hell did you do now?"

Erik's eyes kept skittering to his men at the front. "My turn is up."

"By whose command? Yours or his?"

"Who is speaking? *I am.* Now go," Erik yelled at him, tapping Marcus' horse on the rear with the tip of his sword, the animal whining loudly before running off to the back of the lines.

Erik rode hard and fast to the front, reaching down to pierce the chest or back of several Englishmen, and possibly Scots, who were doing more than holding their own. He slid off his horse and moved through the chaos, careful to look for those who would mark him the enemy.

The sound of two English men talking jovially while fighting, their backs together, caught his attention. Erik strode over, his sword swinging powerfully at the large giant in front of him. The English bastards were carrying on conversation while fighting. Fools.

"Did you see him?" the bald one asked.

"See who, you fool? I just see the blood of dying Vikings around us."

"Erik of Denmark."

"Who? Who's Erik of Denmark?"

"He's the famous Saxon. The prince among thieves."

"A bloody prince? Sod him. I'll wear his crown on my arse."

Erik moved quickly, cutting down another man in front of him. He stood in front of the arse-wearing-crown man. It took three strokes of his sword to bring the two chatty males to their knees. He ended their rumors of his demise. His men where not thieves, and he never acted the role of prince.

He looked around him. Men lay dead before he could reach them, their bodies ravaged as more men on the field fell. They were losing ground. The raging fighting continued, the sound of swords clanging against another filling the air alongside the soft groans of death finding new hosts. The trees opened and more English men piled through, another wave of fighters joining the battle.

Erik lifted his voice to the skies. "Archers move!"

The light from the sun was clouded by the number of arrows that flew above their heads, the fighting stopping only for a moment as the arrows met their intended victims. Screams and shouts lifted to the sky before the men took back to fighting. Erik battled through the crowd, his sword in one hand and his ax in the other. Blood coated his face and clothes, his fingers dripping with the life of those around him. His arms swung without ceasing, the enemy pressing in on them and seemingly him specifically.

It became hard to tell who part of his battalion was and who were not. He lost himself to the heat of war, killing for fear of being killed. He spun around, his axe catching a young boy in the throat and nearly severing his head. The boy dropped, his small kitchen knife falling beside him. Erik stared only a moment, the horror of his own actions dismissed because there was simply no time for remorse in the middle of hell's war.

His soul screamed and he lifted his eyes heavenward as he let out a fierce battle cry he was sure shook the ground beneath them. His declaration seemed to fuel his men on further, the tired soldiers raring up again to fight like everything depended on it – because it did.

He moved backwards putting his bloody fingers in his mouth, whistling loudly. His horse rode up beside him. He climbed on top of her, his eyes witnessing atrocity. The men were moving into the large seaport city, their swords still raised and the cry of battle still on their tongues.

"NO! Hold the line!" Erik yelled as Marcus rode up beside him.

"Halfdan's given the command for annihilation. It is the reward for our chastity last night."

"Reward?" They hadn't even won the battle yet!

"Where a seed is left of descent, soon grows the need for revenge. Is there anything greater than the driving desire to right oneself and find justice for the slain?"

"Your words are lofty and full of shite. They mean nothing to what Halfdan is offering. You're an idiot, cousin." Erik growled at Marcus and clicked his heels, riding hard and fast into the city. He moved in beside the large giant from a few nights before, two girls pressed between him and a wall as he tore at their clothes, his teeth sunk into the flesh of one of their shoulders as the girl screamed in pain.

He was a demon, a monster from hell. It was no wonder the world would come to know them not as men, but as the spawn of Satan himself. Erik rode toward him, extending his sword and cutting deep into the back of the large man's neck, his head lulling forward before he slumped dead before the girls.

Screams and cries filled the large town, Erik tried rushing toward the sounds. They seemed to be coming from everywhere. Small children and beautiful women lay dead in the streets, their gowns once white now crimson as their life blood stained the walls of the city and colored the mud of the streets.

How had this happened? *Halfdan.* The bastard was mad...

"Erik. Come." He heard the sound of his commander, the cries of the people just around the next corner beckoning for help and yet he knew that to deny his Sire twice in one day would be punishable for even him. Halfdan had done this because of Erik.

Because of me. He turned, riding toward the small group of men who stood around his commander.

A cocky smile hung on Halfdan's face. "Go to the field and instruct those there we are taking all weapons and silver. Loot as much as you can, and we will be meeting you on the northern end of town. We set up camp there."

He looked Halfdan in the eye, the darkness staring back at him nothing new, but a desolate realization washed over him, nearly knocking him from his horse. The man had no soul. He didn't care for Denmark or the crown. He wanted power for himself. Nothing more.

"Put a stop to the killing of innocent, or I will." Erik narrowed his eyes.

Marcus turned his horse and headed back out of the city, yelling over his shoulder, "I'll take care of it."

"You answer to me, boy!" Halfdan snarled. "Watch your tongue or I will cut it out. Your beloved father isn't here to save your arse from my wrath. You can be labeled a traitor as much as the next fellow."

The eyes of the men around them diverted as if attesting to the fact they heard nothing, saw nothing, wanted no part of the controversy existing between the two men.

Erik swallowed his frustration. The minute he found rest he would send a message to his brother. Nathaniel needed to be alerted. They were dominate and demanding, rulers and pillagers for this new world, but they weren't the bastards that Halfdan had them believing they were.

"Anything else?" Erik bit out between clenched teeth.

Halfdan pressed him with his stare.

Erik sat quietly as if he hadn't a care in the world. He could not thwart the cries and horror going on around him. His death would not help the dying, but he could prevent further destruction in the future. He would right this wrong and they would still win the war. Things were about to change and no one would expect his reaction.

Tonight he would take command of the army. He barely glanced at Halfdan before he rode off toward the field, his blood boiling, and his heart racing. If there was a salvation to be offered to his men, to his cousin, for his own character, it would need to come soon for the battle was assured to become bloodier as the fighting turned inward.

They would bow before someone, but it wouldn't be Halfdan in the fields of victory. It would be him. He didn't want this cup, but if it had to be so, then it would be. He was created to lead. Somehow this greedy bastard had moved in. Erik knew this was a defining moment. His father would be proud of his decision.

An example had to be set – and Marcus was going to help him. He just didn't know it yet.

Chapter 10

Linzi

Martha left as the afternoon sun pulled toward the western slope of the sky. Linzi, still dizzy from the drink and her shoulder on fire, hugged her friend and slowly trudged into the house, shame sitting heavy on her from her actions. What was she thinking? Her father would surely kill her.

Speaking of which, she needed to check on him again. She walked into his room, a soft hiccup leaving her lips as she reached over and touched his head, jerking her hand back at the scorching heat. "Oh no... no..." She rushed to the kitchen and grabbed the pail of water and a washcloth, her lunch pushing from her stomach into her chest. She felt like she was going to be sick from the fear threatening her. She needed Kenton. She didn't know what to do for a fever other than cold water and medicine they didn't have.

The sheets were soaked, her father's color more flushed than the red of her new rose ink marking. She knelt beside him and bathed his head, his eyes opening only slightly as he muttered something. She leaned in and pressed her ear near his mouth. "What Da'?"

"Wa—her."

"Water?" She jumped off the bed, her shoulder burning from the large marking Martha had spent the entire afternoon making. She ignored the discomfort and raced to the small kitchen, fumbling with the glasses as one fell on the floor before her and cracked in half. She kicked it aside and grabbed another. Once filled, she raced back, spilling half along the way. Weight spread, she leaned over to cradle her father's head in the crook of her elbow. She lifted him up, pouring the water down his throat slowly. He choked and she pulled back, cursing herself for not being more careful.

She helped him lay back down, his eyes opening a little more as he spoke, his voice a raspy whisper. "Linzi, I-I need med'cine." He swallowed painfully. "I'm 'eeling ill."

It meant going to town. On her own. She picked up the rag, leaning in and wiping at his head. "Of course, Da'. I'll go to the lady at the edge of town." The lady liked the bread she made and there was a loaf from yesterday that was meant for tomorrow. She'd trade eating a day for the safety of her father. "I'll take bread to her and..." Linzi let her voice trail off as her heart caught a scared rhythm.

She leaned over and tilted her head, sighing with relief to hear his ragged breath moving in and out of his parched lips. She had to be fast. Night was drawing close and it wouldn't be but a few hours of sunlight left for her trip. She pulled the blanket around him, worried at the dampness of it, but knowing there was nothing more she could offer.

In the kitchen she wrapped up the bread and also took the remaining cheese. She would give the old woman anything she wanted in order to get herbs and medicine for her father. Tomorrow vegetable broth would fill her father's belly. She would have to boil it in the morning.

She paused by the door to the house and looked out across the field whispering a small prayer before closing it behind her and scurrying toward the well-worn path to town. She wished like hell her brother was with her, but knew God had a plan for each of them and this was hers. She would grow stronger somehow in the midst of this.

She reached up and touched her shoulder, flinching as tears filled her eyes. What a stupid, stupid idea. Hopefully He would forgive her for marking up her body. She huffed out a sad breath.

It wasn't God who she was mostly afraid of gaining disapproval from.

It was her father.

The door to the small house hung open, creaking against the push of the wind, as Linzi approached. The scribbling on the sign out front giving credence to an apothecary living there. She knew how to read, her mother had taught her long ago. She stopped at the opening to the home and leaned in, the darkness almost blinding as her eyes narrowed. "Oye! Is anyone here?"

A hacking cough made Linzi jump. "Come in, child. Leave the bread and cheese on the table when you enter."

Linzi touched the bag hanging limp to her side, her offering concealed and yet the woman had spoken truth she could not know. Chill bumps covered Linzi's arms and legs as she stiffened, the room void of movement or noise. She stood just inside the door, her eyes finally focusing on her surroundings. A small array of candles lit up the room from the back wall, the place not hosting one window. Rows of shelves lined with dried herbs, trinkets and other strange things in small jars that Linzi refused to let her eyes linger upon.

She pulled her bag from her shoulder and crept cautiously toward the small table, pulling out the bread and cheese and laying them down upon it. Unwrapping the items, Linzi held up the small towels which covered the food moments before and turned toward the woman. "Would you like me to leave the cloth or might I take it back to my mother?"

"Yer Mum 'as none the need, but you may take them, lass."

Linzi turned around, her questions all answered as to the power of the witch-doctor who sat a few feet from her. The old woman with her grey and white hair pulled into a tight knot, stared fixedly on Linzi, her wrinkles showing many years of being in the sun.

"Sit." She pointed to the small table before her and Linzi moved as instructed, her hands dropping to her lap and fidgeting as fear rushed through her. She needed medicine, nothing more. To be in the presence of someone who could only see what belonged to God was an abomination. She bit at her lip, trying to look the woman in the face and not quite able to keep eye contact.

The woman waved her hand. "I'll get ye the medication yer looking for. Yer father will regain 'is health wit' four pills, nothing less... nothing more, or 'e will not." She stood stooped, not much taller than when she had been sitting.

Linzi gave her a simple nod, her eyes jerking around the space as the woman moved painfully slow around the small room.

It wasn't but a few minutes later the old woman stood before her, hand extended to Linzi. "Take it! It'll not bitechya."

Linzi stood, thankful to be on her way without having to linger in the strange smelling, creepy cottage. She reached out, her palm open for the health being offered.

The woman reached out and grabbed Linzi's wrist, holding her grasp tightly with one hand and dropping four large white pills into her open palm with the other. She leaned in and stared hard into Linzi's eyes. Her breath rank like a dead animal. "Sometimes the truth of character lies hidden well beneath the call of duty."

Linzi swallowed hard and blinked a few times, confusion washing over her. She nodded and the woman simply stood still, her grasp rough and unrelenting. The woman's accent seemed to have changed into a clear, crisp tongue. "Thank you," Linzi murmured clearly confused.

"Sometimes the truth of character lies hidden well beneath the call of duty."

"I understand," she said, even though she had no idea what it meant. "Thank you for your willingness to trade." Linzi pulled her arm back and the woman instantly released her.

As she hurried toward the door, the woman whispered more truth than Linzi cared to hear. "No you donnin', but ye will, chil'. Ye will."

Why could these things not have happened while Kenton's still home to deal with them? Year after year of health and everyone doing just fine and the moment he leaves to fulfill his dreams, all hell breaks loose. She slipped the pills in her pocket and huried toward the small bakery in town, her mother's best friend, Sara, owning it. Linzi was reminded each time she stopped by that if she were ever in town to come by and get a treat. She most certainly needed one that night. She had a long walk and short time to get back to her father. Images of him crawling on the floor to get water, thrashing helplessly in his bed as he called for her, and many others filled her tired mind.

She slipped into the small shop, a silver bell shaking on the backside of the handle.

Sara moved away from the large hearth and smiled. "Well, I'll be. Look who's here to see me!" She clapped her hands, flour littering the air as the portly woman walked around and scooped Linzi into a tight hug. "Let me look at you, child."

"Hi Mrs. Sara. Nice to see you again." She didn't have time for pleasantries but they were required.

"You're not a child anymore. What happened?"

"I suppose all your treats over the years finally caught up to me?"

The woman laughed and moved to put her arm around Linzi's shoulders. "You suppose right. You're as beautiful as your mother, a spitting image of her, I say."

"Thank you." The idle chatter needed to stop. "I've come to town because Da' is ill and needed medicine."

Sara moved toward the hearth again, working to pull out three loaves of steaming hot bread. She shook her head, concern spreading on her features. "What's the matter with the old boy?"

"It's fever and it's quite bad." Linzi pressed her lips tight together a moment to stop them from trembling. She would not be weak, she did not have time for it. "I covered him up and bathed him in cold water, but nothing seems to be working." She reached into her pocket and pulled out pills, extending her hand. "I came to town to trade for these."

"Where's your brother?" Sara frowned and Linzi could almost read her thoughts: *Pretty girl travelling the roads at dark in a dress to tight and short for a proper lady.* "Haven't you heard that the Vikings are drawing near, child?"

"He's gone to fight, Mrs. Sara." Linzi put the pills back in her pocket and pressed herself near the wall as the door opened to the shop and two large men walked in, each taking a turn to look Linzi over.

Sara snorted. "What can I get ya?"

"Loaf of bread for the wife, please mum."

"I'll take two and make one of them with the raisins and sugar like you did last week, Sara."

"Will do. Take a seat and don't mess with the girl or I'll bake you into a loaf next. Got it?"

The two men chuckled, nodding their acceptance and making their way toward the door, sitting down and paying attention only to one another. Linzi couldn't help but listen in on their conversation, Sara depositing a large slice of hot bread smothered in butter before her.

"Jeffery told me that he could see the smoke from his property. They must be burning the damn towns as they move through."

"Aye. I was told the streets of Northumbria were running red right into the sea."

"I wouldn't be surprised. My boy asked to join the fight this morning and I told him like I've told him a million times. The damn Vikings don't fight fair. They are evil and will kill, steal and destroy anything they can get their hands on."

"How do you know if someone is a Viking?" Linzi asked, both men turning to face her.

"They have a spear or knife and a dead body hanging off it," one of them laughed.

Sara poked her head up and scolded them. "Answer the girl's question. She needs to be prepared like we all do."

"Sorry, lass," the older man offered, shrugging his shoulders and sitting back.

The younger one turned and motioned with his hands. "They usually wear furs, and their bodies are honed for fighting, helmets made of dead men's sculls. They're tall and strong, so much more fit than us."

"Especially you, George," Sara called out from behind the hearth. It made George's friend laugh.

Linzi smiled, her question yet to be answered. "There are no markings or anything to label them as Vikings?" Her stomach growled loudly from the delicious aroma of fresh bread baking in the ovens.

"Most of them have a Triquetra just beneath their ear. It's a sign to each of them in battle as we all look the same, I guess, when bloody and beat up. Or dead."

"What's a Triquetra?" Linzi tried to repeat the word and butchered it.

"It looks like three teardrops placed together." The older man stood and walked toward Sara. "Give me a writing piece to show the girl."

Linzi took a bite of the bread in front of her as the man moved toward her with a small piece of paper, drawing the symbol for her.

He set it down and tapped the center of it with his pencil. "You see that and you need to run like hell, lass."

"Pray you don't ever, hmmm?" Linzi picked up the paper and slipped it in her pocket before walking toward Sara. "I need to go. Thank you for the bread. Thank you for the information," she said to the men.

Sara grabbed her by the elbow. "Hold up a moment, lass. I'll not let you go hungry." She ignored Linzi's attempt to say no. "I've already paced you a load. And don't give me no grief about it. I know yer situation and I'm praying for all of you. Come to town next week and I'll give you another."

She slipped the warm bread into her carrier bag and thanked her mother's friend.

The younger man standing, went and opened the door for her. "Tell your father he needs to train you to fight, to at least punch a man in the soft parts of his body, not just the jewels. Like the rest of us, you need to prepare, girl. The fight is coming this way."

"Where are the soft parts?" she asked, her eyes wide as her heart constricted in her chest. She was willing to fight, to find the harder parts of herself and bring them out, but someone had to share wisdom of what to do.

The man pointed to his eye, then his nose, then his crotch. "Punch them in the eye, square in the eye, or the tip of the nose. If that doesn't work, grab a hold of his bits and squeeze like hell. Kick 'em there if you have to. Kick 'em till blood foams at his mouth."

She nodded, terrified of the man's words and disconcerted it might be something she might actually have to do one day soon. Steeling her horror deep inside of her and saving it for further analysis later, she slipped out into the street, the sun racing its final dance toward the edge of the sky. Now was not the time to enjoy her trip back home, and as such, she ran the majority of the way.

Linzi arrived to her small house an hour later and rushed in, paying no heed to the sweat that ran down her back. She poked her head into her father's room relieved he hadn't moved from the bed as her visions had shown. He was snoring softly and in the next same position as when she had left.

She quickly set the bread on a small cutting board and poured her father some water. She was thankful his condition was growing no worse or better. She woke him and helped him to swallow one of the pills she'd picked up for him. Her hope for him eating anything died as he slipped back into unconsciousness.

She pressed her hand on his chest and prayed for his health and their safety. She stopped by the kitchen and picked up a potato bag from town and the biggest kitchen knife she had. No one was going to help her get ready, but that didn't mean she couldn't help herself.

She walked to the edge of the trees and dropped everything, walking back to the house to get a small digging shovel and returning to her supplies. She bent down and chipped the earth with the small shovel, working to fill the bag beside her with dirt enough to create form. She stood and bent her knees, groaning at the weight of the bag as she pulled it up and tied it to a long-hanging branch. Yelping, she let it go and moved back, the rope having sliced her hand for her efforts.

Linzi reached up and tied her long red locks into a knot before picking up the knife and lunging up, her wrist flicking as the blade laid a small tear in the bag. It wouldn't last long, but she refused to go back to the house for rest until she placed the blade perfectly in the face or groin of her make-shift attacker.

The sun dropped over the edge of the earth and she exhaled loudly, the bag dropping to the ground for a long cut at the neck of her would-be enemy. Sand spilled on the ground before her and she hit her knees, tears rising in her vision as she pushed them back down.

The Vikings were coming and she alone could protect their home and her father.

There was no time for fear.

Chapter 11

Erik

Erik approached Marcus at the edge of the city, his cousin coated from head to toe in a mixture of blood and sweat. His beautiful horse beneath him shuddered and danced around as if the creature was too pure for the atrocity in which it witnessed.

"Where are the men?" Erik asked, his voice filled with venom.

"They are bathing in the sea. It's over. We've claimed the city."

With how many casualties? How many English escaped in the forest? This was no victory in Erik's opinion.

The look on his face must have annoyed his cousin. Marcus shifted on his horse and said, "I've spoken to the men and calmed the rage within them." He shrugged when Erik said nothing and started to move past.

Erik reached out and pulled him to a stop, their horses touching. "Something's not right here." He frowned, his resolve ever more determined. "You'll help me make it right, or you'll regret the day your mother released you from her womb. Do you understand?"

Marcus sniggered, pulling the reins free from Erik and leaning in close to him. "There isn't a day that goes by I don't regret the day I was born. You've the world before you and yet you act nothing more than a lofty fool. Do not speak to me of greatness or deceit. Your father was the epitome of both. What of Nathaniel? Is he worthy of the crown given him?"

"Watch your mouth, *boy*."

Marcus met his challenging stare, the look on his macabre face far too calm for Erik's liking. "That I shall. This land is ours and the filth on it will fall to my sword or my shaft." He grabbed himself, his vulgarity nothing new and yet sickening all the same. "I'll be no part of righting anything." He didn't give Erik a second glance as he directed his horse back toward the city.

Erik watched him, darkness sitting around them. His cousin did not see what was happening. He was falling prey to gluttony and greed. All the men were. They were turning into Savages, not Vikings.

He clicked his heels on the belly of his horse and reached down to rub his fingers through her mane as they moved through the field of dead bodies. He instructed the looters to make haste. Sitting in the open fields was dangerous. The English could be lying in wait. There was always a chance of an additional battalion showing up – fueled by the death of their countrymen and angered beyond reason.

The ground lay covered with death, the night rolling in fast and the heat finally dissipating. Erik rode to the edge of the forest unafraid to risk his own life, narrowing his eyes to look for additional men. Nothing moved other than the small creatures of the night. He turned away from the forest and stared at the highlands they would soon be marching toward. The lights of Scotland lay ahead of him. He relaxed momentarily, his shoulders slumping as he leaned forward and pressed his chest to his horse's strong back, his arms holding her tightly.

Images flashed behind his closed eyes; women and children killed, how many had they raped? He forced his eyes open. Bile rose in his throat and he swallowed it down, his hatred for the situation threatening to consume him.

The sound of horses approaching caused him to sit up. He started to turn as something caught his attention – the soft whistle of an arrow rushing through the air. His heart constricted just before the arrow plunged through his shoulder, just above his heart or in it, he couldn't be sure. A second arrow hit him in the stomach. He groaned at the pain, his body starting to slump as consciousness drew nigh.

The world faded as his mare whinnied, afraid of her master's distress and sudden lack of control on top of her. She took off galloping into the forest as Erik fell onto her, his arms losing strength as darkness squeezed out the light.

Stopping Halfdan would not happen tonight. He tried to focus his disorganized trains of thought, but agony seared through his body.

Something was terribly wrong... the arrows had come from his side of the camp.

He couldn't have been more than nine, his father forcing him and Nathaniel to take lesson after lesson in the art of battle. It seemed a torrential waste and yet arguing with father would likely land him with a bruised buttocks and ego to match. He huffed softly, his older brother smiling as he picked up the small wooden sword that had been crafted just for him.

"Pick up your sword, Erik. You never know if father is watching. Give it full effort and let's see if you can beat me this time. Stop acting as a babe attached to mother's teat." Nathaniel motioned toward the ground with his weapon, Erik looking over at his for a few moments before finally moving to pick it up.

Nathaniel popped the back of his legs, the slap stinging badly. Angered, Erik jumped up and attacked, the pain of his brother's playfulness sparking something inside of him. He hated to be hit and his father made sure to hit both of them more times than necessary in Erik's young mind.

He swung with all his might, his thin arms not developed like Nathaniel's. His brother held his own, but Erik maneuvered just right, the opportunity to kick Nathaniel's feet out from under him arising. Erik took full advantage of it, his body poised perfectly to dive for his brother's falling figure. He pressed him to the ground and sat up, holding his sword with the tip of it against Nathaniel's throat and growled softly, "Don't mock me ever again."

A clapping sounded from somewhere behind them. "Bravo, bravo. The diplomat is once again pinned by the little commander in chief." His father walked out, the long purple robes of royalty adoring his tall figure. He reached down and offered his hand to Erik, pulling him up and putting an arm around his shoulders. "Leading people is in your blood, boy. You will one day be a force to be reckoned with."

They were probably the kindest words his father had ever said to him. Erik straightened with pride.

"Yes, but it will be I who is King, right father?" Nathaniel asked as Erik turned and sneered at his brother. He could care less about being king, but his brother used the very fact all the time to rub in his superiority.

His father laughed again as his mother walked into the room, her long dark brown mahogany hair draped across her back. She was the most beautiful creature in all the world, her heart pure and her voice soft like an angel's might be. Erik broke from his father and walked to his mother, the woman pulling him into a tight hug as his father responded to Nathaniel's cry for attention.

"Yes, son. You will be King one day if you don't let someone beat you with a wooden sword. Or a sword of any kind. Dead is dead." He scowled down at his older son. "Then, should anything happen to you, your brother Erik will take your place."

"I don't want it." Erik turned and moved from his mother's hold.

His father looked ready to release his backhand. "What do you mean?" he roared. "To be King is the highest honor. You lead our people. You become the beating heart of the country." The look on his father's face a stark warning not to argue.

What nine-year-old boy understood a heartbeat or what his father rambled on about? "I don't want to be stuck in this castle all the time. I want to go into the forest to hunt for deer, explore the world, see the ocean. If you're a king you can't do that." He crossed his arms. *A king can't fight in a battle. He has to wait at the back to see if he's won."*

His mother chuckled. *"Being King gives you the freedom to do whatever you like, dear."*

"That's not true my Queen." His father walked over and ruffled Erik's hair. An action Erik didn't recognize and ducked, thinking his father planned to smack him. Nathaniel stood near the door like a dejected doll of sorts. *"There are many things I get to do, but you, my son, are more concerned with getting to fight. The King does not fight, but the commander has victory painted behind his name in crimson blood at all times."*

"Jorgen..." His mother warned of something, but of what, he knew not. He didn't want to fight to death and see the horror of battle, but telling his father that would end poorly for him.

His father pushed Erik toward the door. *"Go. Play in the fields I always see you wandering about in."*

Nathaniel stopped him just before he left, leaning over and whispering roughly, *"I'll always be King. Then you will have to fight for me when I tell you to. There will be no time for hunting or farming. That is for free men. You... you will never be free as long as I reign. You will always have to watch your back."*

Erik pulled away from him, his brow creasing as he grimaced toward his brother. *"Then I shall simply kill you and become King myself. I am the fighter of the family. Better watch your back, big brother."*

He hurried from the room, knowing Nathaniel, even though he was older and taller, could never run as fast as him. He sprinted away with his head held high, a smile on his lips at the pure horror on Nathaniel's pretty-boy face.

Erik forced the memory and fog inside his head to clear. He came to, his hands pressing against the horse beneath him, the beast having stopped at the edge of a large field. His vision swam as he tried to sit up, a loud groan leaving him. He'd been hit. Twice. He tried to steady himself enough to get his fingers around one of the arrows, the thin wood protruding from his chest and another lower down. Closing his eyes and swallowing painfully, he struggled to breathe. He carefully released himself from his chain mail and ripped at his shirt, dropping pieces of it as the horse swayed back and forth, the animal most likely thirsty and exhausted too. Luckily his mare had not been hit also.

"Shite," he muttered, reaching up to break the wood where it entered him low in his stomach. A long scream lifted to the sky, the pain of moving the damn thing almost his undoing. He lay back down against his horse as he built the strength to make attempt on the second arrow. He finally broke the other one, blood filling his mouth as he bit down on his tongue far too hard. He spit and reached around to his back, his arms shaking from the effort of moving at all. Carefully he found the pointed end of the arrow, his left shoulder numb from blood loss.

He closed his eyes and whispered a prayer to the gods. Pressing down hard on the horse he pulled with all of his might, the arrow slowly leaving his skin and then finally coming out into his right hand. He screamed again, blood pouring down his back and the front of his chest as the world began to fade before him. He needed to get the other one out of his back, his organs most likely punctured. Death would surely come for him. The ground below him began to spin. An Englishman or Scot Highlander could easily come and pick him off. Either way, he wanted to die free of the current impalement that tore at his insides with every breath he took. He would not die from a Saxon's hand.

He looked up to the heavens and reached behind him, using both hands to grab the small stick that protruded from his lower back. The horse moved and then paused, as if she understood her movement might kill him. He breathed in quickly and pulled, blood pouring from the open wound on his stomach. It took all his strength for one more hard jerk before the arrow finally pulled free. Erik screamed again, agony ripping at the very essence of his core. He fell back down on the horse and lamented for only a moment.

He would never have land or a wife. He would never have a boy to teach to fish or hunt, to covet and one day show the ways of peace to. He would die here in a field, his men wondering where he was, his death treacherous. He felt his weight shift and went with it, his body dropping from the horse to the soft green grass below. He rolled on his back and groaned, his death deserved for all the life he'd taken.

The stars offered peace. He breathed in a painfully shallow breath before releasing himself back to unconsciousness.

Chapter 12

Linzi

There had been screams just outside her window the night before. She was sure of it and as the morning sun rose, she burrowed deep into her covers, terrified for what she might find. There was an expectation that any minute someone might break down the sad excuse for a bolt that sat on their door, the piece of wood holding the Vikings out nothing more than a twig to their efforts.

She shivered, though covered in sweat from hiding underneath so many layers of wool. Linzi lifted her hands from the covers and examined them, her knuckles busted and raw from hitting the bag outside too many times. She touched her palm and winced, the long red line across it still tender from her rope burn. She wasn't sure how much her efforts would pay off should she encounter a Viking, but she knew one thing.

It was going to hurt like hell to hit him.

Hopefully the Vikings would wait another day or so, just so her wounds could heal. She sighed and got out of the bed, tiptoeing around the house and listening for the sound of anyone approaching.

Nothing.

Gathering another pill for her father, she went to pour a glass of lukewarm water for him. The pitcher was almost empty, the small amount she gleamed from the jug not nearly enough to help him get the medicine down. She cursed softly, fear beckoning her to make it work.

She straightened, annoyed at herself for the silly thoughts and being scared of the night shadows. If the Vikings were at her door she would damn well know it. They would be raising a fuss and instilling terror in everyone. The devil didn't sneak into a village, he burnt it down and reveled in the screams of the innocent.

She went to check her father, relieved to find him sleeping. He was still hot and feverish but he was alive. The mug she had left beside his bed lay untouched. There would be enough for the pill this morning, but nothing more. Not even enough to wash her face.

Shaking him gently, she roused him enough to have him open his mouth and take the pill. More water spilled down his chin than into his mouth. At least the pill went down without him choking. He mumbled from the terrible heat and Linzi was grateful when he fell back. He thrashed until she put the last drops of water onto a cloth and laid it gently on his forehead.

Assured he slept, she pulled a shawl over her shoulders and moved toward the door, tucking the water jug under her arm. Carefully she pulled the small piece of wood from the door and opened it, sticking her head out as the early morning rise of the sun painted the sky in brilliance. How much she would love to enjoy the rest of its rising up on the hill beside her mother's grave, but danger seemed to lurk in the air around her.

Leaning out the door a little farther, she let her eyes scan the horizon, nothing out of the ordinary catching her attention. She moved just outside the door and closed it behind her, stopping and holding her breath to simply listen.

"You're being ridiculous. Stop being a sissy and go get the damn water," she growled softly, angry with herself for letting fear paralyze her. Her father and brother treated her like an innocent flower, but the lovely roses spilled across her shoulder and the top of her breast would tell a different story. She made that solemn promise to herself. She would protect them as much as they had protected her.

A smile touched her lips and she slipped off into the field toward the well. She walked quickly through, convincing herself it was simply from concern for her father.

She thought about Luke and imagined how much fun it was going to be learning more about him, falling in love with him. He was cute and seemed to be sweet. Kenton never spoke a harsh word about the boy before. Some of his friends were just rascals altogether, their womanizing already had begun in their teenage years.

She smirked at the thought. How would Luke feel unwrapping her the first time and seeing the signs of rebellion painted across her? She reached up and slipped her hand beneath the opening of her gown, the skin still raised from having Martha create the design. What had the world come to?

Her thoughts turned to the boys now in battle. Had they fought? Were they dead already? What would happen if neither Kenton nor Luke returned? If her father died?

Linzi moved to the well, working to get the water up and ignoring the ache in her hands and arms. She pulled the bucket up and poured the water into the jug. She froze at hearing the soft huff of something behind her. She yelped, turning and preparing for the worst. She hadn't brought her knife, all she had was a bucket of water and a half empty jug.

A beautiful brown Arabian Mare moved around the edge of their property, the horse eating at the grass, but whining softly. She could see the efforts of his labored breathing, his condition hurting her heart. She dropped her shawl and carried the bucket, walking cautiously toward him, her body bare beneath the thin cloth of her night clothes. Surely no one would approach and if they did she would simply run.

She approached the animal slowly, one hand extended as she whispered to it. "It's okay, girl. I just want to give you a drink." She reached out and ran her hand down the side of the horse, her fingers returning stained with what looked like blood. A scream rose in her throat, but she swallowed it, reaching down carefully to wipe her hand on the wet grass. The poor animal had been through enough. She didn't need her scaring her with the shrill of her scream.

She held out the bucket, the water splashing up the side and hitting the horse. She drank fast and furiously, the poor creature panting as she worked to get as much water as she could. Linzi moved back, the horse moving toward her as she walked back to the well and pulled up more, giving the horse another round of watering. Finally the animal backed up, her large eyes closing for a moment as if exhaustion had finally taken its toll.

She would need to wash the poor thing, but first she needed to get dressed and tend to her father. Reaching up, she took the reins, carefully pulling as she spoke to the animal. She always had a natural way with the creatures. Her brother teased her about it as a child. She walked the exhausted beast back to the house and tied her up. She'd have to clean her and let her go free. Surely whoever she belonged to would be looking for her. She was far too beautiful not to. She was well cared for. She tilted her head and looked over the beast, seeing past the blood and dirt. She was not like the farm horses from around here. She was larger and... Saxon.

Her heart leapt into her throat. She could be setting herself and her father up for death by invitation. She hurried into the house, taking care to get her father more water and hoping he would lie quiet. He could do nothing to protect himself if Vikings came crashing through the house. Her best hope would be for them to think him already near death and leave him.

She would change after she washed the poor creature. From the window she could see her eyes closed and her breathing labored. She could not leave her in distress. She needed care now.

Linzi rushed out of the house. She stopped suddenly as she scanned the field and hill by her mother's stone. Fear froze in her chest. She was sure someone lay out at the edge of the field. The rider? Possibly a Saxon?

She took a tentative step out in the field, the body of the person still a distance away. She crossed her arms over her chest and tried to think of what to do. If she helped him and he was a Viking then he would kill her, but if he wasn't and she didn't? She couldn't fathom letting someone die. The man might already be dead.

She walked into the house and grabbed her kitchen knife, her hand aching at the action of simply holding it.

Courage would have to be her companion, because encountering a Celt was the last thing she believed she would survive. She walked slowly at first, the fear of whatever might come slowing her, but before long she was jogging, the need to help an injured soul overriding her sense of self-preservation. She stopped a few feet from him, his short blonde hair matted to his head with dirt and blood. He lay on his stomach, his face turned from her, but the vision of his exposed back told her two things. He was hit with arrows which were gone, and he looked to be a Saxon.

Long muscles lined either side of his spine, his tanned skin smooth and hairless. By the color of his hair he wasn't belonging to her people or those just south of them. She needed to turn him over to check for the small symbol. It might be an old wives tale, but if he had it then she knew for sure she needed to finish whatever her people had started with him.

"He might already be dead," she whispered, and hated how much she enjoyed the strong slope of his back and upper shoulders. She crept around him, dropping her knife as she moved closer to see he'd been hit twice. Surely he'd not pulled out his own arrows. She looked up quickly, trying to assess if he had companions nearby. He might be bait for any unsuspecting idiot to come and try and help.

She stood up, turning in a circle slowly before moving back toward him. The subtle movement of his upper back told her that he was still alive, but barely. She steeled her courage and rolled him over, moving away from him with a soft yelp on her lips. He rolled with her efforts, but lay completely limp. His handsome face came on display, the soft curve of his lips drawing her first. A light dusting of hair covered his cheeks and chin, but she couldn't tell the color from the stain of war on his face, neck and chest. Long eyelashes lay on his high cheekbones, his neck thick and chest defined from his shoulders to the long abdomen muscles that hovered just above his breeches.

She chided herself as foreign emotions rolled within her. This was what lust felt like. The desire to see if he was as powerful as he appeared to be.

"He's half dead and you're going to finish him," she whispered, not giving a care in the world that she was talking to herself. Her sanity hung in the balance and terror waited just at the edge of her thoughts. She had to move fast or she'd not have the willingness to do this thing.

She realized she dropped her knife when she'd come close. As luck would have it, the stranger had an axe and hand knife on his belt. She pulled the intricately carved handle from its hilt and held it in her hand. It seemed to carry strength and begged to draw life from its tip.

Staring down at the stranger she realized cutting his throat would be the fastest way for him to go without much suffering. She bent over, trying to figure out the right angle before resigning herself to climbing on top of him. Her breath caught in her chest as she moved onto him, straddling his lower stomach careful to sit low enough to not disturb his wound. It might cause him to waken from the sudden pain. She felt the crest of his hip bone high against her thigh, the material of her thin night dress doing nothing to stop the sensation. She had never been this close to a man. Her hair fell down around her face with all her movement.

"God give me grace for my actions," she whispered and lifted the knife to the left of her body, her right hand holding it so tightly her arm shook. One quick swipe and he'd be flayed.

One swipe.

She screamed when his hands moved up her thighs, strong fingers digging in as his hips shifted, pressing his body to the center of hers. She started to move but he locked her to him, his eyes opening with heaviness. She stayed poised to kill him, his movements leaving the small symbol of the Vikings on display below his left ear. Blue eyes the color of the ocean stared at her, the smile on his lips sexy, and promising things she couldn't begin to imagine.

"You're a Saxon – a murderer, a bastard. You have to die." She lifted up on her knees, her eyes wide and heart pounding so hard she expected it to rip from her chest.

His words came soft, spoken just before he fell back into unconsciousness. "Sometimes the truth of character lies hidden well beneath the call of duty."

The world stopped for a moment, the words of the witch washing over her. She swung with all of her might, her body lunging forward as she buried the knife deep.

~ The End ~
Celtic Rune
Book 2
Coming May 2015

Note from the Author:

Thank you for reading Celtic Viking!
If you enjoyed the story, please take a
moment to leave a review on the site you
downloaded the book on so others can
find Celtic Viking.
I love hearing from my readers so feel
free to connect with me on Facebook or
any other social media (you'll find my
links everywhere in the book, lol)
Thanks again,
Lexy Timms

xxx

More by Lexy Timms:

The Saving Forever Series
Part 1 is FREE!
SAMPLE CHAPTER EXCERPT INCLUDED!

Charity Thompson wants to the save world, one hospital at a time. Instead of finishing med school to become a doctor, she chooses a different path and raises money for hospitals – new wings, equipment or whatever they need. Except there is one hospital she would be happy to never set foot in again, her fathers. He hires her to create a gala for his sixty-fifth birthday. Charity can't say no.

Now she is working in the one place she doesn't want to be, attracted to Dr. Elijah Bennet, the handsome playboy chief, and trying to prove to her doctor father that's she's so much more than a med school dropout.

Why would she try to put together so many things that are clearly broken? Or will she realize in time that they just need to be fixed?

The University of Gatica Series
The Recruiting Trip
Book 1 if FREE!
Book Trailer: http://www.youtube.com/watch?v=5FdSZUaJ2q0
Aspiring college athlete Aileen Nessa is finding the recruiting process beyond daunting. Being ranked #10 in the world for the 100m hurdles at the age of eighteen is not a fluke, even though she believes that one race, where everything clinked magically together, might be. American universities don't seem to think so. Letters are pouring in from all over the country.
As she faces the challenge of differentiating between a college's genuine commitment to her or just empty promises from talent-seeking coaches, Aileen heads to Gatica State University, a Division One school, on a recruiting trip.
The university's athletic program boasts one of the top sprint coaches in the country. The beautiful old buildings on campus and Ivy League smarts seems so above her little Ohio town upbringing. All Aileen needs to convince her to sign her letter of intent is a recruiting trip that takes her breath away.
Tyler Jensen is the school's NCAA champion in the hurdles and Jim Thorpe recipient for top defensive back in football. His incredible ocean blue eyes and confident smile make Aileen stutter and forget why she is visiting GSU. His offer to take her under his wing, should she choose to come to Gatica, is a temping proposition that has her wondering if she might be making a deal with an angel or the devil himself.
* This is NOT erotica* It is a new adult & college sport romance.
For mature readers only. There are sexual situations, but no graphic sex.

Heart of the Battle Series
Celtic Viking
Book 1
Celtic Rune
Book 2
Celtic Mann

Book 3

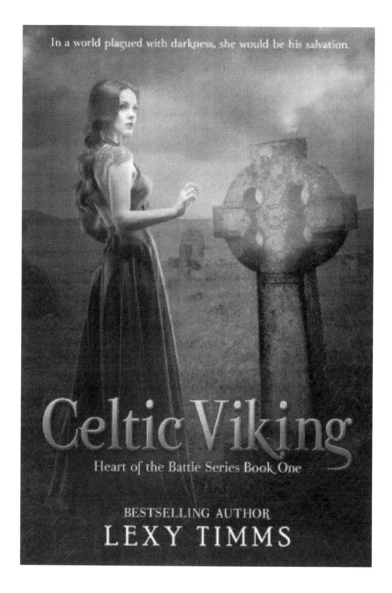

If you enjoyed Celtic Viking,
try Lexy Timm's
Saving Forever Series:

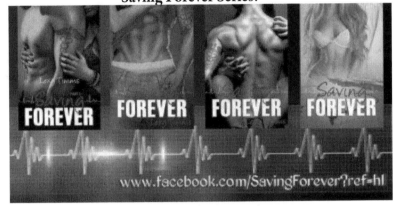

SAVING FOREVER SERIES
Book One is FREE!
Book Trailer:
http://www.youtube.com/watch?v=ABs_uaeEamo
Website: https://www.facebook.com/SavingForever

EXCERPT INCLUDED!

Saving Forever

Chapter 1

"You do realize you have a very unique name for the business you're in?" The doctor smiled and winked at her. His hazelnut eyes sparkled with mischief. "I'm sure you've been told that a million times."

Charity laughed. "My mother must have planned it all while I was in her tummy." She tucked a chunk of her long blond hair behind her ear. It had been six years since her mother had lost her battle against cancer, which had completely changed Charity's career course. The day after the funeral, she had dropped out of medical school and hadn't looked back since. She couldn't say the same about her father. She forced a grin and focused on the moment. "It's even more ironic now that I'm signing a two-year contract with you guys. How shall we put the press release? Forever Hope Hospital hires Charity Thompson as their new Fundraiser Liaison. Kind of a tongue twister, eh, Dr. Parker?"

"Just Malcolm, please. We're working together now. It's in the two-year contract you just signed. It says you are to refer to Dr. Parker as Malcolm only." He held it up, teasing her.

Dr. Parker—er, Malcolm—couldn't be much older than Charity, maybe five years tops. Cropped hair and chiselled features probably made him popular talk amongst the staff and patients. She knew he was single, recently divorced, with no children. She wondered how long it would take a first year or nurse to 'make the rounds' with him. Or maybe he would surprise her and actually be a decent guy.

"As for the press release, I can't wait to see everyone and anyone's reaction. It's going to be a big success. Between the humor in your name and job, your awesome track record for success..." He pointed and in a very kind voice added, "Your beautiful face, plus the fact that your father is *the* Doctor Thompson, I'm not sure we should send the press release to the local papers or to the American Journal of Medicine." He stood and reached out his hand. "I'm teasing again, of course. We're all very excited to have you on board."

Charity stood and shook his hand, making sure to add just the right about of firmness to show her strength and still remain feminine. "I'm excited to get started."

"This hospital needs your help. We're in dire straights. Between the state cutbacks, the simple lack of funds, our long term care ward, and our outpatient surgery floor is anciently outdated, we either need to update or close down. People are starting to skip past us and are driving the extra forty-five minutes to Atlanta General." He shook his head. "You already know this, sorry. I just hear it everyday, a million times a day."

Charity sat back down and pulled her iPad out of her briefcase. "Then we need to get started right away." She flipped to the screen she'd written the list of things she needed from the hospital. "I'm going to need the hospital's financial records, and a calendar of events you already have set up. I'd like to plan a charity luncheon in about six weeks to get the ball rolling. Remember, this isn't going to be fixed overnight. It's a process and two years is the goal. We'll get there."

Vibration from the doctor's cell phone on his desk made her pause. They both looked at the phone and then at each other.

"Continue, please." He glanced at the phone and then back at her.

"You're busy. You need to take care of hospital issues. Why don't I talk to your assistant and check your calendar? We need to pick a day in five or six weeks that you can take a long lunch break." She thought back to his comment about her having a pretty face. "We need to use those good looks of yours and get some lovely high society ladies wanting to spend money on the hospital with the hot doc."

He blinked, surprise clear on his face. "I'm not sure if I should be insulted or pleased. Hot doc?"

She laughed. "Sometimes pretty works and you have to use it." She stood and slipped her briefcase strap over her shoulder. "Sorry, doc, but you're single, good-looking, and funny. I'm going to have to use you as a marketing tool to get a few charities going." She held up her hand. "I promise no cheesy date auctions or prostitution. Just need to use your... your atmosphere to see how awesome the staff and hospital really is."

"I'll do whatever it takes. I love this place and want everyone else to love it as well."

They were going to work together just fine. "You need to go be a doctor and I need to set up my office."

The doctor slapped his forehead. "I almost forgot! Your new office is to the right of the elevator. I've had it cleared and your name's supposed to be up on the glass by the end of the day. I'll get my assistant to show you where and she'll also bring any information you need." He pressed the red button on the intercom phone on his desk. "Amanda, do you mind helping Ms. Thompson?"

A millisecond later, the office door opened and in rushed a tiny, petite lady. Her silver hair in a messy bun held a pair of reading classes stuck on the top of her head. "Doctor Parker, Doctor Mallone is trying to get a hold of you. He needs you in emerg right away." She turned, almost floating like a little fairy. "Ms. Thompson, let's go." She disappeared out the door, her little shoes tapping down the hall.

It felt like being in third grade all over again. Charity raised her eyebrows but wasn't about to disobey Amanda. As she took a step toward the door, a smooth hand touched her elbow.

"She's harmless," Malcolm whispered, his warm breath tickling her ear, "but I've never crossed her." He chuckled as he let go of her. "Good luck."

Charity mouthed a sarcastic *Thank-you* and hurried out the door. She could feel Malcolm's breath cooling on her skin as her long strides slowly caught up to Amanda.

"I had a two-sided desk set up in your office. I also had them set up a bookcase, but didn't know what else you would need." Amanda's words punched out with each tap of her shoes. She stopped in front of a frosted glass door and pulled a key out of her pocket. "This is yours." She handed to key to Charity. "I'm glad you've come. Welcome to Forever Hope. Just let me know if you need anything else." She stood waiting.

"Thanks." Charity realized the woman wanted her to open the door so she hurriedly put the key into the lock and turned it. She pushed the door open and grinned when she stepped inside.

"Will it work?" Amanda asked.

The office was actually two rooms, kind of like a waiting room and then an archway that showed a glimpse of a large, light wood stained two-sided desk. The walls were completely bare except for a fresh coat of pale yellow paint. *Bright without feeling like a hospital.* It gave her an idea. "It's going to be perfect!"

"Lovely. I'm down the hall if you need me." Amanda disappeared out the door.

Charity set her briefcase against the wall by the door and pressed her lips together. She'd done six large-figure multi-million dollar fundraisers but never had an office like this. *Two rooms!*

Racing through the brightly painted white arch, she surveyed the second room. It was a bit smaller than the first room, but both had large window panels to look over the city. Day or night, the view was probably amazing. The two-sided desk had a brand new computer still in its box sitting on the far side, along with a phone already set up. The leather chair behind seemed to beg her to try it out. Well, she couldn't disappoint it.

The soft leather felt perfect under her. She tested out the wheels and tried sliding from one side of the desk to the other. No problem. She slipped her heels off and felt the wood floor against her bare feet. It made her want to dance. *Focus, Charity.*

She pushed her chair away from the desk and went back to the first room to look around. The bright, empty room would make a perfect conference room. Give it a laid back, homey atmosphere and possibly donors would relax the minute they stepped in. She pulled her Blackberry out of the short-sleeved red jacket that went with her black dress.

Maybe a loveseat, definitely a round table, four comfortable chairs, two ottomans, plant, fridge, cabinet to hold glasses, wine rack.

She glanced around. There were three walls to work with since she didn't want to put anything but a low table near the windows. If she painted the one wall with chalk paint, that would be a perfect note-board and would also work as a projector screen for presentations.

A buzzing in her hand caught her attention. She had a call. Quickly saving the shopping list, she then switched screens to check the caller ID. She almost dropped the phone when she saw the number.

Saving Forever
Chapter 2

"Dad!" Her father never rang unless there was an emergency. "Is everything all right?"

"Hullo?" The voice that answered wasn't her father's. It was husky, with a clear accent.

It took her by surprise and sent a shiver down her spine at the same time.

"I'm sorry, is this Charity?"

She scratched her head, trying to recognize the caller. Australian accent? Or New Zealand? "Where's my father?"

"I'm not too sure, actually." The stranger chuckled. "I was just in a meeting with him an' he said he needed to call you. Suddenly he tosses me the phone and rushes off to some code three over the intercom." A slight grating noise echoed through the phone like the stranger was rubbing a five o'clock shadow. "I'm sorry. I don't even know what he wanted to tell you."

"That's okay. He does have a habit of rushing off to save the day. Who is this, by the way?"

"I'm Elijah."

"Hi Elijah, I'm Charity." She shook her head. Was she honestly flirting with some stranger over the phone? Her father's phone on top of it. She really needed to get out more.

"It's a pleasure to meet you." He chuckled. "Well, over the phone anyway."

She smiled. "Not to make you the messenger, but you can let my dad know I've arrived and he can call me when he has a free moment."

"Arrived?"

She absently waved her hand in the air and walked around the room surveying what she needed to do first. Hardware store, the furniture store. "I just started a new contract down here in Atlanta."

"A little warmer than New York at the moment."

"Definitely."

Muffled voices carried over the phone. "I apologize again," Elijah said, "but Dr. Thompson needs me."

"No problem. Have a great afternoon."

"You too."

Charity slipped her phone into her jacket pocket and grabbed her briefcase. She wondered what Elijah looked like. That sexy accent surely belonged to a good looking guy. She rolled her eyes. The guy was over a thousand miles away and she had a new job with a lot of work to do.

Speaking of work. She needed to get a list of past donators, skim through the local papers to find the elite social class. The first group would be women. Doctors' wives and local celebrities. She already had connections to a couple of popular bands that would do charity concerts for her. It was simply a matter of getting dates and plans to coincide.

She headed out of the office and back down the hall to Amanda's office.

Amanda sat behind her computer, reading glasses on the bridge of her nose. She smiled at Charity. "What do you need, sweetie?"

Charity dropped into the chair in front of Amanda's desk. "I need lists. People who have donated to the hospital, anyone big named or wealthy who have been here. Even those who wished to remain discreet. I'll contact them on the down-low but I need names." She went through her mental list of things she wouldn't have access to find. "Has the board made blueprints or hired architecture to design the new wing Malcolm wants to add?"

Amanda shook her head. "I don't believe they have." Her hand slid her computer mouse around and she clicked it a bunch of times. Pages started printing out of the massive computer behind her. "Dr. Parker started collecting data when he was pretty sure you would agree to help us out."

The printer continued printing out page after page after page. That was a good sign. More meant a lot of options and possibilities. "Has Malc—Dr. Parker or any other doctor worked on athletes as well? Anyone from the Braves, or Hawks or the Falcons?"

"I'm sure there are quite a few."

"Does every doctor have a seat on the board?"

Amanda shook her head. "I don't believe so."

Her father was a stickler for every person having their say. He was adamant about all doctors meeting at least twice a year to discuss hospital issues. His hospital would be a success and never be in need of someone like her. It made her very proud of him.

"We'll need to set up a meeting with everyone." She ignored the slightly annoyed look on Amanda's face. Charity had two years to turn this place into a success story and she needed everyone willing to work with her. She knew what needed to be done and it was never easy at first, but that would change. "How about you send me everyone's email address?"

"You can't get everyone to meet at the same time. The hospital would have to close for the day."

Charity smiled. She knew better than to argue. "You're right. I'll have to come up with something that works for everyone." She stood and checked her watch. "I've got errands to run for my office that I want to do tomorrow, and my stuff is supposed to be delivered to my apartment sometime after five today. Gotta jet."

Amanda scooted her chair back and grabbed the massive stack of printed paper. "Do you want me to bind these for you?"

"That would be awesome. I'll start going through them tomorrow then."

"Good luck."

"Thanks. I think I'm going to need it."

"And Charity?" Amanda set her glasses on the top of her head.

"Yes?"

"I'm glad you here."

Amanda was full of surprises. Charity grinned. "Me, too."

Saving Forever
Chapter 3

Trying to balance her groceries and case of water in one hand, Charity slipped the key into her apartment door with the other. She had met the moving company earlier. It hadn't taken long to unpack, and all that was left were five clothing suitcases in her bedroom. She then ran out to grab food for dinner and breakfast in the morning.

She kicked the door shut with her foot and glanced around. It was a studio apartment with a double sized living room, which opened to a modern kitchen. Light grey stained wood covered the floors and the two rooms were painted a soft white.

Very bright. And very empty.

That had been done on purpose. A leather antique psychologist couch was set against the far wall, mirrors covered another wall, and a high tech stereo system took up most of the space on the last wall. The only remaining wall had windows and a door to a simple balcony.

Charity slipped off her shoes and padded on bare feet to the kitchen. She set the case of water down on the breakfast bar and quickly put away the groceries. Before putting the water under the table, she grabbed the remote beside the case and turned the stereo on. The tall speakers came to life and Charity reached for a bottle from the case. As she strolled to her bedroom, her fingers tapped the music's beat against the plastic water container. By the time she reached her room, she was full-out dancing.

She changed into tights and a sport top, then headed back to the living room. She had been dancing since she was six. Her mom had encouraged her to try every form of dance and she loved them all. Somehow, all the different types of dancing had rolled into her own artistic interpretation and she was phenomenal at it, but very few people knew. It came in handy during the galas and dinners if someone asked her to dance and she could surprise guests.

Dancing was her workout, her stress reducer, her fun time and her down time.

An hour and a shower later, she started cooking dinner. Munching on a carrot, the little red light flashing on the phone caught her attention. She flipped her screen on and saw several emails from Amanda with attachments, an email confirming the paint and furniture for her office would be delivered in the morning, and her father had called about ten minutes prior.

He hadn't left a message so she pressed the button to call him, putting him on speaker so she could continue cutting vegetables.

"Dr. Thompson."

"Dad, it's me." Charity tried not to roll her eyes. He had caller ID so he knew it was her.

"Charity. How can I help you?"

She shook her head. "You phoned me earlier and tried again a bit ago. I was in the shower and just saw the missed call. I assume you wanted to talk to me." No 'how are you doing?' or 'how's Atlanta?'.

"Oh yes. I did. I was going to have my secretary call but I knew you'd say no if she asked."

Charity set the knife down. She didn't want to stab her phone. "Nice, Dad. I really appreciate you starting a phone conversation on the negative. Why don't you just ask me what you need and I'll let you know what I think?"

"Fine. I'm turning sixty-five next year." He paused.

"I know." A strange thought crossed her mind. She never assumed he would, but what if... "Are you retiring?"

"Hell no! I'm more than competent as a doctor, probably still better than most of the doctors I know."

No lie there. He was one of the best doctors in the country, even had a hospital named after him. "I didn't think you would, but why the phone call just over six months before your birthday?"

"The hospital wants to make a big deal with it. I guess they need to. I said I would take care of it since I don't want it to be about me. I want the focus on something else."

She had no idea where he was going with this.

"I was wondering..." He swallowed and a quick sigh echoed through the phone. "We'd like to hire you to do the party."

She blinked in surprise. He hated her job and always made sure she knew how disappointed he was that she'd dropped out of med school. "I'm not a party planner."

"You don't organize parties and plan big events?"

Good point. "I do but they are for hospitals wings, additions, equipment. The galas are to raise money for non-profit issues hospitals need." Not some retirement party where the birthday dude wasn't even retiring.

"Exactly. That's what I—what we want to hire your for. To make money for some new equipment at the hospital. My milestone age marker is just the excuse to do it."

Charity tapped her fingers against her lip as she thought. It was actually a very good idea. Everyone knew and liked her father. He never made a fuss about himself publicly so a lot of doctors from all over the country would fly in for the night. Plus the countless patients whose lives he had saved. It was a great idea.

So why her?

"I've just signed a two year contract down here in Atlanta. I can't drop everything for them for six months and help you. That wouldn't be fair."

"I'm not expecting anything spectacular. It's fine. I'm sorry I bothered you."

Giving up that easy? That wasn't her father. That competitive side of her kicked in. He didn't think she could do spectacular? Boy was he in for a surprise. "How much money are you hoping to raise?"

"It doesn't matter."

"How much?"

"A hundred thousand would cover half the price of the equipment in the emergency room."

"Your gala could easily raise quadruple that."

He scoffed. "Really?"

"Easy." She thought about going back home. Did she want to? Part of her did. The kid in her wanted to prove to her father that she was good at her job. That she deserved to be patted on the head and told she'd done a good job. That her career change hadn't been a bad choice. "Look. If you can handle working on the weekends for this, I can do it. The flight to NY from Atlanta is direct. It's only a one night gala. I can work online from here and fly up twice a month or whatever to get it set there." Six months wasn't that long.

"You'll do it?" The surprise in his voice made her smile.

"Sure. I'll have to come up this weekend to find a location. It's going to be a time crunch, but it'll work."

"Perfect." Scribbling of a pen made its way through the phone. "I need to go. Duty calls."

"Life of a doctor. I'll meet you at the hospital Friday afternoon sometime. I'll email you my flight details."

"I can send someone to pick you up."

"Don't worry. It'll be easier if I rent a car."

"Sounds good." He paused. "And thanks, Charity."

"You're welcome."

She stared at the phone after her father hung up. What had she just gotten herself into?

Saving Forever
Chapter 4

Once off the plane Charity waited for her bags and then picked up her rental car. The mid-size car she hired wasn't available so the young teller bumped her up to a Mustang. Blue. Sapphire blue. She laughed out loud in the parking lot when she tossed her suitcase and bag in the trunk. The weekend might actually turn out to be fun.

The week itself had been busy. She'd painted the office, had it decorated, went through the email list, and set up a luncheon with Malcolm for Monday. They needed to go over a few plans and she also needed to meet with the board next week. Juggling the two jobs would be interesting.

She drove straight to the hospital and parked in the visitor parking section. The newly designed hospital almost looked inviting. They had torn down the older hospital two blocks away months ago. The grey outer walls had loads of windows and sections of it spread like rays of sun around the nucleus.

The warm heated air brushed the cold autumn air away as she stepped though the sliding doors. She headed for the elevator but slipped into a restroom just before. She washed her hands and looked in the mirror. Her ponytail had slipped down so she grabbed two chunks of hair to tighten it. The pony band snapped and shot off like an elastic.

"Crap!" Charity searched through her purse for another one but found nothing. She ran her fingers through her hair and tucked a few strands behind an ear. It would have to do. Except now she needed to touch up her makeup. Little makeup worked with a ponytail but not with her hair down. She grabbed a lip gloss and added eyeliner and mascara. She stepped back. Dark jeans and white button up would have to do.

She squared her shoulders and exhaled a long breath. "Please give me patience and don't piss Dad off," she mumbled before leaving the bathroom. She hit the elevator button and the far door slid open. *Perfect timing.*

An older couple walked off together and she smiled at them before stepping into the lift. Leaning against the wall, a tall glass of hot water stood in medical scrubs. Short, dark, slightly mussed brown hair, bright blue eyes, and a sexy five o'clock shadow held Charity's gaze a moment longer than what was considered polite. She quickly turned and pressed the sixth floor button. It was already lit up. Hot muscle guy had to get off on the same floor.

She closed her eyes and silently sighed. She should have looked at his badge instead of his face. The thought of his chest made her wonder what he might look like with his shirt off. She forced herself to open her eyes and stare straight ahead. *You're being ridiculous. Cute guy and you act like a thirteen-year-old boy-crazy kid.*

She turned around and smiled, willing her eyes to stay on his face, not cruise down and then back up. "Are you a doctor here?"

"I am." The stranger smiled but offered no more information.

Sexy smile. She tried again. "Is your office on the sixth floor?"

"It is."

Did she detect an accent? Her eyebrows furrowed together. Had they met before? She would have definitely remembered. She glanced down at his hospital tag just as the elevator came to a stop. *Dr. Bennet.* The door slid open so she turned to step out. She stopped short when she realized she didn't know where to go.

Dr. Bennet walked right into her and grabbed her elbow so she wouldn't fall.

"I'm so sorry. Are you a'right?"

Definitely an Australian accent, or something by there. "It's my fault." She shook her head. "I'm not sure where Dr. Thompson's office is. Last time I was here they were still finishing this floor."

Two young nurses walked by. One winked at the doctor. "Hi, Elijah." The other nurse elbowed her. "Oops. Hello, Doctor Bennet." The two disappeared into the nurse's room.

Elijah? Charity remembered her dad's phone call when she'd spoken to him. "I'm Charity." She held out her hand. "I'm Dr. Thompson's daughter. We spoke earlier this week on the phone."

Elijah reached for her hand. His warm, strong fingers enclosed around hers and he smiled at her again. "I remember. You're much more beautiful in person."

No wonder the nurses were so friendly. He was a lady's man.

"I can take you to your dad. I was just about to see him myself."

"That'd be great." If he was a flirt, she could flirt, too. "Lead the way."

He pulled his phone out of his chest pocket and checked his messages. "I just need to call downstairs to see if my x-rays are done." He headed past the nurses' station and down the hall.

Charity followed and admired his lean muscular shoulders that dipped into a firm derriere that looked fantastic in hospital pants. She felt her cheeks grow warm. *There's nothing wrong with appreciating a fit body. Get over it, girl.*

"...Thanks. Have someone send them up to the sixth floor review room. I need them quick." Elijah tucked his phone back in his pocket. "Sorry about that. So, how long are you in town to see your dad?"

"Just the weekend. He wants a fancy to-do for his sixty-fifth. He's asked me to plan it."

"I'm sure you'll make it amazing." He scratched the stubble on his chin. "I have to admit, I Googled you after we spoke on the phone. You're quite the successful donor-fundraiser... party planner... thing." He shrugged and made a confused face. "I don't know what your official title is."

"Neither does my father," she teased, "but at least he knows what I do or he wouldn't have called." She noticed the wing they'd been walking down now had expensive wooden doors. The first office had her dad's name on the plaque, and across the hall was Elijah's name. "You must be pretty special to have an office right here." *By my dad* is what she wanted to say but held back. Her opinion of her father was not shared with fellow doctors. He was *the* man. The Dr. Scott Thompson. Lifesaver super-hero.

"The chief gets the next best office." Elijah dropped his head a bit and grinned like a little boy. "Sorry, just trying to impress you."

Charity blinked, surprised at his honesty. "I'm impressed. A little." She pretended to shrug. "You're pretty young to be chief. I'd ask who you had to sleep with to get the job, but since my dad's in charge, I don't really want to know."

Elijah's head tilted back and he burst out laughing.

The door to her father's office swung open, probably from the sound in the hallway. "Charity!"

Chapter 5

A bit more grey in his hair and a little more tired, her father still commanded power. Years of hard work and respect earned from success gave him that posture. He was one of the best doctors in the country, even at almost sixty-five. He would always be distinguished and handsome. Charity sometimes wondered why he hadn't remarried since her mom passed away. He'd probably had a lot of offers.

She hadn't seen her dad in over a year, almost two years. Two Christmases ago she had flown home to spend the holidays with him. Christmas day ended in a big row right after they had gone to the gravesite to drop some flowers off on her mother's stone. She'd left early the next morning, not even sure if her father was still in the house or already gone to the hospital. Last year she made up the excuse she had to work so she wouldn't have to fly home. She felt guilty, but guilt was better than fighting with a man who couldn't be wrong.

They still called each other once every two or three weeks and never discussed the fight. He had made the first call and she had called him the next time. It continued until he called earlier this week. Four days and two phone calls had broken the pattern.

"Dad!" She awkwardly stepped forward to shake his hand at the same time he leaned over to hug her.

"I trust your flight was all right?" He stepped back so she could come into his office.

"It was fine." She stepped through, absently tucking a strand of hair behind her ear.

Elijah followed her into the office. She'd momentarily forgotten he had brought her down the hall. "Why don't I let the two of you catch up and I'll chat with you later, Scott."

"No!" both Charity and her father said at the same time.

"I mean," said her father, "I want your opinion on what I'm hiring Charity to do for the hospital. As chief you also need to sign off on it."

Charity glanced back and forth at both men. Did her dad seriously mean that, or was he just as afraid as her to be in the same room alone together?

Elijah checked his watch. "I can really only stay a moment. I have surgery in thirty minutes and need to scrub in with a first year. It's a cardiothoracic, so I'm not leaving my attending in charge."

Her father harrumphed. "Right." He clapped his hands and walked around to his desk and sat down behind it. "Why don't you meet Charity and me for drinks after?" He stared at Charity. "What's that place we went to before... the Threaded Cork? Yes, that's it. Meet us at the Threaded Cork when you are done." It wasn't a request.

Elijah nodded. "Sounds good. You're treating then, right?" By his smile and relaxed stance, it was obvious to Charity that he wasn't intimidated by her father. Elijah just earned a new level of respect from her. He smiled at her, and just as he turned to leave he winked, then strolled out the door.

An uncomfortable silence filled the room after the door closed. Her father cleared his throat as he rested his fingertips against each other. "I really appreciate you being willing to take this on."

"It's not everyday your father turns sixty-five." She crossed her legs and then uncrossed them. "Do you want this gala to be a dinner or just a party?" Part of her dreaded planning it, but another part really wanted to show her father how good she was at her job.

"What do you think?" His thumbs tapped a steady beat while he waited for her answer.

"Well, it all depends on how you want the evening to go. Do you want to focus on raising money for the hospital, or your birthday, or the fact that you're stepping down?"

"I'm not stepping down." He straightened against the back of the chair.

Charity had to make herself resist the urge to let her eyes roll upward to the ceiling. "Okay, but from a professional standpoint, I need to know what the theme is going to be. If I don't ask you and set the wrong theme, you are going to hate it."

"Right. Sorry." He relaxed his straight posture by a tenth of a degree and ran his fingers through his hair. "I built this hospital so we could be a leader in research and innovative surgeries. I plan to keep up the research end and help run the board, but Dr. Bennett is the chief now. He's good at his job." He looked Charity directly in the eye. "Lousy at staying away from the women. Ask the nurses or first years or anyone who seems to look good in a skirt."

Charity burst out laughing. She couldn't help it. "Are you jealous, Dad?"

"Just warning my head-strong daughter."

"And I wonder where I got that from."

"Yes, well okay then." He checked his watch and stood. "I really don't care what you do with the evening. I'd just like the focus to be on the hospital. I figured my sixty-fifth would be a good excuse to throw it. If it makes money, great. If not, that's fine too."

"Sure." She knew what he meant. He wasn't expecting much from her. Well, she would surprise him. Six months to plan it would be tight, but if she flew up two or three weekends a month she could make it a great turnout. "What time do you want to meet at the Threaded Cork?"

"Meet? I just thought we'd drive back to the house together and go from there."

Charity's cheeks grew warm. "I, um, I booked a hotel room. I just thought it'd be easier for me to work and –"

"Right," he cut her off. "I have some work here to do as well. Why don't we aim for six o'clock then?"

"Six o'clock it is. I'll have some ideas and check out some possible venues. We're going to need to pick a spot as soon as we can."

"Perfect." He went to the door and held it open for her. "I'll see you there."

Charity pressed her lips together as she bent to grab her purse. Six months of being uncomfortable seemed like a prison sentence at the moment, but she owed it to her mother to make the effort.

After leaving the office, she took the stairs down to the main floor and let the cool wind soothe her face. Heading to the parking lot, she grinned when she found the Mustang. Maybe a new outfit to go with the car might be something to cheer her up. She could shop and brainstorm at the same time.

Charity turned the blow dryer off as she finished straightening her hair. She'd managed to find a simple black sleeveless dress at Michael Korrs and a pair of black shoes with just the right amount of heel to look sexy without looking like a stripper. She wondered how Elijah would be like outside of the hospital. She mentally kicked the thought out. Tonight's dinner had to do with her father's fundraiser gala. Her dress was fun but also completely business suited. Eye shadow followed by mascara and a dab of lip gloss and she was ready to go.

She stuffed her iPad into her briefcase and her jacket. Its length matched the dress's – perfect without even trying.

Parking downtown turned out to not be as easy. Friday night in a busy city had everyone and their neighbour looking for a parking spot. Charity drove the block around the Threaded Cork three times before getting slightly lucky and spotting a couple getting into their car. She flipped her blinker on and carefully parallel parked the car. Good thing she hadn't gone with the higher heels, as she had a few streets to walk. Tossing her keys into her purse, she stepped out and walked around the car to grab her briefcase.

Someone whistled. "Wow. That's quite the ride."

Elijah. The accent was hard to miss. She smiled, locked the car, and turned around. "Rental place gave it to me. I honestly didn't ask."

"Let me get that for you." He offered his hand and took her briefcase, slinging it over his shoulder. "You must have made quite the impression to the car clerk."

She laughed as they started walking. "He was kinda young. You have to troll around for a parking spot as well?"

"I actually took the subway. Surgery went a bit longer than I thought, so I showered and changed at the hospital."

She glanced down at his outfit from the corner of her eye. Black pants, fitted button up, and she caught a whiff of a delicious men's cologne. "How did the surgery go?"

"Quite well, thank you for asking. The patient is a young woman in her early forties. She had a small hiccup while on the table but we fixed it, and her heart, in the end." He slipped his hands into his pockets.

"You could have stayed at the hospital if you preferred." She said it just to be polite but was more than pleased he had come. Talking to her dad over dinner on her own seemed daunting.

"And miss seeing you dressed to the nines?" He pretended to clutch his heart. "I'll have to get mine checked out when I get back to the hospital."

"You are really, really cheesy." She laughed, despite the corniness.

"A bit too much?" He grinned and small lines crinkled near his eyes. The look was striking.

"It suites you," she replied honestly.

They turned the corner and headed down the last block length to the Threaded Cork.

"So what is it your father wants to hire you to do for the hospital?"

Charity pushed the fallen strap of her purse back on her shoulder. "To be honest, I'm a bit surprised he called me. He doesn't quite agree with my career choice." She waved her hand, embarrassed to be sharing that information with him. "I mean, he's turning sixty-five, and since he is *the* Doctor Scott Thompson, he knows he has to do something big with the ol' milestone number. He'd rather make the emphasis on the hospital than him."

"It's a great idea."

They reached the entrance to the Threaded Cork and Elijah handed Charity her briefcase and then held the door open for her. The outside of the building had not changed since the last time she had come. It had the old heritage appeal but painted with modernist colours and flare.

Dim inside, Tiffany lights hanging above each solid table clearly showed who sat at each location. Her father was already sitting at a place near the far wall. The back of the restaurant where the bar and wine tasting area had been built was quiet. It would fill after the dinner rush.

Charity led the way to the table and Elijah pulled her chair out for her. Surprised, she managed to remember her manners and whispered, "Thanks."

"Did you two drive together?" Her father raised a single eyebrow. How he had ever mastered that ability had always bugged Charity, even as a kid. She tried for hours to make only one brow go up.

"I drove." "I took the subway." Elijah and Charity spoke at the same time and then laughed.

"We met just outside," Charity added.

The waitress came by with three wine glasses and two bottles of wine; one red and one white.

"I took the liberty to order a bottle of each," her father said as he looked at the menu. He smiled at the waitress. "What are your specials tonight?"

After they ordered and filled their wine glasses, Charity pulled a folder out of her briefcase. "I scouted a few places and we have a few options." She flipped her iPad case open and slid through her apps until she found the one she'd set up. Tapping the screen, she slid the tablet so both men could see the hall set up. "I thought about doing the party at the hospital. You have the large gymnasium you could turn into a high school prom setting." She suppressed a giggle when both men's eyebrows mashed together at the same time. "Hey, it may sound cheesy but it would be a huge hit. The entire idea behind prom," she made small circles with her hand, "what happens after prom. You know, the whole package. Laugh all you want, it will get donators giving."

The smirk on Elijah's face told her he liked the idea; the forced smile on her father's told her otherwise.

She slid the tablet picture to another floor diagram. "This is the old downtown concert building. It's heritage but has been completely revamped inside. It's like a Phantom of the Opera kind of building. They have this amazing chandelier that was restored. It sparkles even when the lights are dimmed." She snapped her fingers. "We could make the evening about diamonds. Make it a platinum, gold, and white evening."

Her father topped up Elijah's and his wine glasses. "Quite the opposite of venue ideas."

"Well, you gave me next to nothing to work with so I'm using every angle to make your evening something you want." She took a long sip of her red wine, embarrassed at her response and that her voice had risen. Elijah's piercing blue eyes watched her intently but his face revealed nothing. "Sorry. It's been a long, busy day and—"

"You always get a tad snappy when you're hungry." Her father waved his hand. "Elijah, what do you think?"

Charity glanced back and forth at the two men. She had three more possible locations. Her father had already made up his mind. He just didn't want to admit he liked it. She knew her first choice would be a no. It had only been to throw the idea of having the gala in the hospital. Her father would have wanted to do that but it wouldn't be the success it could be. The cheesy suggestion would turn off any thought of having it there. The other possibilities were, well, possibilities. The diamond heritage would be very classy and right up her father's alley.

Elijah folded his hands on the table. His long fingers and smooth fingernails looked tanned against the white of the tablecloth. "As much as I would love to experience an American prom, I believe the Diamond place is more suitable for your birthday."

Charity smiled. "Agreed. What about you, Dad? I also have some other ideas."

The waitress arrived with their dinners and set their orders in front of them.

"In lieu of your snap turning into a roar, I settle for the Diamond thing as well." Her father set his napkin on his lap.

Inhaling the delicious aroma of roast chicken, Charity felt giddy. Possibly from the wine, the hunger, or getting her dad to agree to the location, she elbowed him lightly. "Wonder where I get that from?"

Chapter 6

They ate their meal with light conversation, Elijah and her dad doing most of the talking. They discussed hospital issues and a number of upcoming surgeries. A sense of wistful dreaming filled Charity. She had chosen to drop out of medical school and had absolutely no regrets, but that didn't mean she didn't miss it. For one millisecond she wondered if she had stayed, graduated and become a doctor, would she be sitting at this table talking with them about upcoming surgeries and post-op procedures?

She poured her second glass of wine of the evening and glanced around as she savoured her first sip. The lights had dimmed and the crowd had changed to a slightly younger generation. The bar was getting busy and the noise level had risen a few notches.

"… You two stay, finish the wine. I'll go and pay the bill."

Charity blinked and focused back on the conversation at the table. Her father stood and rested his fingers a slight moment on her shoulders as he stepped past her.

"Can you come by the hospital tomorrow or do you have an early return?"

She nodded. Her flight didn't leave until one p.m. "I can stop by. No problem. Thanks for dinner tonight."

"My pleasure. It was good to see you." He turned to Elijah. "You'll walk her to her car?" When Elijah nodded he added, "I'll see you at the hospital shortly."

She shifted in her seat so she could watch her father leave. He walked straight, smiled pleasantly at the hostess as he paid the bill, and disappeared out the door, never turning back to wave or glance at them. Her lips pressed tightly down. The next six months were going to be a challenge. How her mother stayed happily married to the man was beyond her understanding.

"What is it with the two of you?" Elijah's husky voice broke through her thoughts.

Darn that accent is sexy. He's gotta know it. Charity picked up her wine glass and took a sip. He'd probably prefer to talk about himself than the un-comings and lack of goings between her father and her. "You're from Australia, right?"

"New Zealand," he corrected.

"What made you decide to come to America?"

Elijah settled back in his chair. "Scholarship. Opportunity. And maybe just a little bit of running away from home."

"Running away?" *Interesting.*

"My mother's very much into the society club, the yacht club, and about any other club which exhibits social status. It seemed a good time to try something new."

Charity smiled teasingly. "Sounds pretty prestigious. I hardly doubt you needed a scholarship then."

Elijah grinned. "It fit the part back home and it looks good when you show up in med-school as a foreigner on scholarship. You earn a bit of respect before you start."

"Really?" She let her cheek rest against her hand and enjoyed the guilty pleasure of letting her elbow rest on the table. Her father would be cringing if he were still here. "I'd have thought it would've made you work harder to get the respect." She enjoyed another sip of wine and realized she'd almost finished this glass. She had better slow down or she wouldn't be driving home. She moved her head slightly so she could lean her chin against her palm. His backstory sounded interesting. "What made you want to be a doctor?"

It didn't seem possible, but Elijah's eyes lit up even more. "I had no idea what I wanted to do in high school." He shrugged. "I mean, if I asked my fifteen-year-old self what my plans where, I'd have said sports. I played varsity cricket in university so I started in kinesiology. My anatomy professor in first year talked me into being on the cadaver team. The team consisted of about ten students who cut open the Jane and John Does to teach the other students during class time. I was the only first year, and after ten minutes I knew it was where I wanted to be."

"Cutting up dead people?" She hoped her forced straight face wouldn't give her teasing away. "That's a bit serial psychopath sounding."

"Touché." He laughed. "It's weird, though, it just came naturally. All of it – the dissecting, the anatomy and physiology, like my brain knew it even though my subconscious did not."

"And you still enjoy it?"

"Every minute," he said without hesitation.

"That's very cool. Natural talent in medicine and surgery isn't easy to find. No wonder my father picked you as chief."

"Dr. Thompson is a great doctor. I'm honoured he hired me. When he said he was stepping down and wanted me to take over as chief, I'd be stupid to say no. This hospital is easily one of the top ten in the country. I get to do surgeries most hospitals would never risk and surgeons can only dream of. The other thing about Scott Thompson Hospital is the atmosphere. It's great. Everyone loves being here and that, in turn, helps the patients." He picked up his glass. "Sorry to ramble."

"Don't apologize. It's something you love."

He clinked his glass with hers. "Cheers to that." His elegant fingers rhythmically tapped against the rim of his glass. "I've been here five years now and don't recall seeing you around."

For three months straight, six years ago, I never left the place. That was before all the new construction and the renaming of the hospital to honour her father. "I've been by. You just probably never noticed me."

"I'd have definitely noticed."

She raised her eyebrows but didn't respond. *Was he flirting with her?*

"How long have you been raising money for hospitals?" He shot her an innocent look. "Not to sound clueless but... I have no clue what you do or how you can make a living out of it."

"There's money in this. Some for me, but the best part is that I get to spend other people's money to make more. I've been doing this about five or six years now. In America, Canada, and England. It's all about the money." She couldn't resist bantering him. "That's my job: raising money to pay for all these new wings you doctors want. So you guys can make loads and loads more money off those one-of-a-kind freaky surgeries."

He pointed a mocking finger at her. "This from the girl driving a Mustang."

"It's a rental! They gave it to me because they rented out all the cars from the size I reserved."

"Sure, that's what your cover story is." He chuckled, a husky, throaty one which sent little wrinkles by the sides of his eyes. It was very pleasant to watch and listen to.

"You're trouble."

"That depends..." His eyes locked with hers.

She enjoyed the last bit of her wine. "On what?"

He also took a sip of wine before answering. "On what kind of trouble you're looking for."

Charity watched him. Handsome, smooth, and so definitely a womanizer. He had probably already broken strings of hearts. Should she answer his question and open the doors to a chance of mischief? Did she need that right now? Did she want it? She did but not tonight. Flirting was a safe kind of fun. She had never done the one night stand thing and setting this gala up for her father meant she'd be back and forth here and constantly running into him at the hospital. Things between her father and her were awkward enough; she didn't need to add more to it. She pretended to check her watch.

"I should actually get back to the hospital." Elijah seemed to have read her thoughts and knew what to say. "I want to check my patients' charts from the past two hours. Plus I eventually need to get some sleep. I've had two nights on-call and another big surgery going on first thing in the morning."

"Ouch." She straightened and covered a yawn with her mouth. "Sorry. Been a busy week on my end also."

He helped her slip into her coat, his fingers accidentally brushing her neck. Her skin tingled on the spot where he had touched. Charity rubbed her scarf to try to erase or at least dampen the effect. She collected her briefcase and purse.

Elijah pointed to the half full bottle of white. "Almost a sin to leave unfinished."

"I won't tell anyone if you don't."

"Our little secret then?" He winked at her.

They walked to the exit, Elijah leading the way, and then holding the door for her. Outside they walked side by side. The brisk evening sent little puffs of air out of their mouths and noses. Charity was glad she'd brought her scarf. She stuffed her fingers deep inside her pockets.

"Where are you working now?" Elijah asked after a moment of comfortable silence.

"Atlanta. I just started a new contract this week."

"They don't mind you are working with another hospital at the same time?"

"I haven't mentioned anything because it's not a conflict of interest and I wasn't exactly sure what my father had in mind. It'll be a bit busy, but I can do most of the work here on weekends."

"So you'll be up here quite regularly then?"

She nodded. "I'll be up next weekend, and then probably two weeks after that I'll come up again. Whatever it takes to set it up."

"The Atlanta job, is it similar to this one?"

"Not really. The contract we just signed is for two years. That hospital needs a new wing and a lot of expensive updates. It's not in bad enough shape to tear it down and start over but their other option—hiring me—figured out a way to get the place thriving again."

"It's interesting."

"Not really. My job is to basically find innovative ways to fundraise. To get people to want to give away a lot of money."

"Do you only work with hospitals?"

They turned a corner and a gust had Charity catching her breath. "Wow, it's windy. And to answer your question, right now I'm booked with just working with hospitals."

"So there's a queue to see you." He elbowed her lightly. "Why am I not surprised? How far are you booked ahead? Three months? Three years?"

She blushed despite the cold. He was flirting with her again. "Actually at the moment I don't have anything confirmed after Atlanta. Two years is a big commitment. Most places have their goal set for six months, maybe a year tops. I keep saying I'm going to take a break after I finish one project and before I jump into the next. It still hasn't happened. Maybe I'll finally go on a trip somewhere or a cruise or something." She stared ahead and didn't look at him. She couldn't believe she had just told him that she wanted a vacation. Could she sound any nerdier?

"I haven't been out of America for about five years now. I'm due for a holiday as well."

"You haven't gone home?"

"New Zealand? I planned on going last year but then got hired as chief so I didn't feel it was the right time to go."

They reached her car. "So you're a procrastinator as well?"

"I have my moments."

They both smiled and she fished around her purse for her keys. An awkward moment ensued when she didn't know what to say or do. Should she get in the car? Shake his hand? Hug him? "Do you want a lift to the hospital?" She unlocked the doors using the key chain clicker.

He watched her, his gaze moving left to right like a slow pendulum intently staring into her eyes. "Tempting, but I should probably walk. Then I'll just catch the subway." He held out his hand. "I had a lovely time, Charity Thompson."

Tempting? Weird. It's just a ride. She reached out and shook his hand, part of her relieved, part of her extremely disappointed. "Me too. Have a nice evening, Dr. Bennett."

He waited for her to get into the car and start it before he began walking away.

This is the end of the Excerpt from
Saving Forever – Part 1

CELTIC VIKING   133

Saving Forever Series:

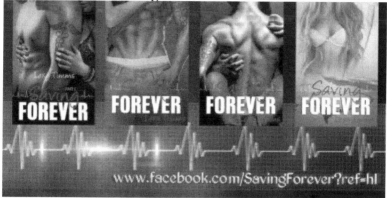

SAVING FOREVER SERIES
Book One is FREE!

The Recruiting Trip

Excerpt

Book Trailer:
http://www.youtube.com/watch?v=5FdSZUaJ2q0

UNIVERSITY OF GATICA

UNIVERITY OF GATICA SERIES
The Recruiting Trip
Book One is now available!

This is Book 1 of a 5 book series

DESCRIPTION:

Aspiring college athlete Aileen Nessa is finding the recruiting process beyond daunting. Being ranked #10 in the world for the 100m hurdles at the age of eighteen is not a fluke, even though she believes that one race, where everything clinked magically together, might be. American universities don't seem to think so. Letters are pouring in from all over the country.

As she faces the challenge of differentiating between a college's genuine commitment to her or just empty promises from talent-seeking coaches, Aileen heads to Gatica State University, a Division One school, on a recruiting trip.

The university's athletic program boasts one of the top sprint coaches in the country. The beautiful old buildings on campus and Ivy League smarts seems so above her little Ohio town upbringing. All Aileen needs to convince her to sign her letter of intent is a recruiting trip that takes her breath away.

Tyrone Jensen is the school's NCAA champion in the hurdles and Jim Thorpe recipient for top defensive back in football. His incredible ocean blue eyes and confident smile make Aileen stutter and forget why she is visiting GSU. His offer to take her under his wing, should she choose to come to Gatica, is a temping proposition that has her wondering if she might be making a deal with an angel or the devil himself.

* This is NOT erotica* It is a new adult & college sport romance.

For mature readers only. There are sexual situations, but no graphic sex.

UNIVERSITY of GATICA SERIES
The Recruiting Trip
Faster

Higher

Stronger

Dominate

Citius, Altius, Fortius

The Recruiting Trip

Prologue

UNIVERSITY OF GATICA

From: Coach Anderson (C.Anderson@gatica.edu)
  Date: Sat, November 1, 2015 at 12:34PM EST
  Subject: GO REDCOATS!
  To: Aileen Nessa (hurdlesrock@gmail.com)
  Hi Aileen,

  I am so excited to contact you again. Since we last spoke in September, I have been looking forward to this chance to get to know more about you. You're an amazing athlete, extremely talented and fun to watch. You have a great attitude, work ethic and passion for our sport. I know you would be a great fit with our program. I hope you know how excited I am about you as a potential student-athlete at University of Gatica.

  I know you are getting tons of pressure from other universities, most of which want an early verbal commitment but I hope you hang in there with us and that you give yourself the time you need to make the best possible decision for yourself. I believe you have the talent and ability to not only gain admission to Gatica, but be a future leader in our program and an impact performer on our team.

As we discussed early in September, the best weekend for an unofficial visit to campus would be February 10-12. We are hosting an indoor meet that weekend and would love it if you had a chance to see the Red Coats in action. Of course, if that doesn't work we will host you any time that's convenient for you.

Coach Maves, the sprint coach will be communicating with you regularly via email to share information about Gatica. If you have any questions or would like to chat, I am always available by email or phone.

I look forward to hearing from you soon.

Best wishes,

Coach Anderson

Coach Anderson

Head Coach, Woman + Men's Track and Field

c.anderson@gatica.edu

The Recruiting Trip

Chapter 1 Excerpt

"Aileen... N-Nessa?"

She nodded as she swung her back pack over her shoulder. "That's me." A guy jostled past her mumbling something about baggage claim sucking.

The chauffer driver tucked the sign with her name printed on it under his arm and took her small carryon suitcase. "First time coming to Gatica?"

"It is." She glanced around the airport wondering why one of the coaches at the University of Gatica hadn't come to greet her. It seemed weird. Sort of. She had no idea what proper protocol was. Were coaches required to meet recruits when they arrived? Or was a shuttle service completely legit?

She had been on four other recruiting trips, the last on two months ago in Miami. The sprint coach there had picked her up from the airport, but the university was about fifteen minutes away from the school.

The chauffer led her outside. She dug through her bag and slipped her sunglasses on against the bright sun.

"You here on a recruiting trip?" The chauffer glanced at her. "Volleyball?"

She shook her head. "Track."

"Cool." He loaded the 'U of G Travellers' van. "The memo says to drop you off Wavertree Fieldhouse. It holds the indoor track and the girls' volleyball gym. They have a gym off the track and then a court set up in the middle of the track for games. It's pretty impressive to watch a game courtside or up in the bleachers above the track."

Aileen nodded, pretending to be interested. She couldn't picture what he meant. Her indoor track was a gym at the high school. Basketball, volleyball, badminton or whatever sport was going on at the time shared the gym with her. Her coach happened to be her high school gym teacher and he was awesome. He wanted her to go to Connecticut or Louisiana, somewhere with a strong woman's track program. She agreed.

U of G had been a last minute choice for her final recruiting trip because of their near Ivy League status – and the fact that the super-hot looking male NCAA champion happened to attend the school.

Aileen's best friend, Becky, had dared her to go. She had gone through all the brochures at Aileen's house and said she needed to go on one recruiting trip based on something other than track. Becky had insisted U of G because of the hot guys. Aileen had said yes because of Tyler Jensen.

She had watched him race at the USTAF championships last summer. He had this amazing physique, all muscle with no fat and a six pack which really should be referred to as a twelve pack. However it wasn't his body that always had her staring at him, it was his face. The short, perfectly cropped hair against his naturally tanned skin and those unbelievable eyes.

She had picked U of G in the hopes of talking to him close up just so she could figure out what his eye color really was.

It was ridiculous. Stupid. She knew it, but nobody knew the real reason she had come to Gatica except Becky, and she only knew half of it. Aileen had never voiced her silly crush out loud. Nobody knew, and she planned to keep it that way.

"Ms Nessa?" The grandfather aged chauffeur lifted his foot off the gas. "Are you alright?"

She tuned back into the present and realized they were on the highway. "Sorry, pardon?"

"I was just wondering if you needed a drink. We've got about an hour and a half before we reach Gatica. Do you need anything?"

"No thanks. I've got a bottle of water here." She could feel the heat in her cheeks but refused to acknowledge it. She stuffed her ear buds in and turned her iPod on, hoping it would defer monsieur chauffeur from chatting.

It didn't work.

"So, where are you from?"

She paused hoping he would think she couldn't hear him. When he repeated the question louder, she imagined her mother sitting beside her giving her *the* look. "From Ohio. Bucyrus."

"What event do you do?"

"Hurdles."

"Sprint or four hundred?"

"Sprint."

"Are you any good?"

Aileen shrugged. "Pretty good for high school. Not so sure about university level." She had spent the past year and half comparing her times to NCAA students. If she compared her personal best to last year's outdoor rankings she would be second. Her indoor times this year weren't so great, only because her coach wanted to focus on the upcoming summer and trying to make the World Junior Championships. However she wasn't going to brag to a total stranger. She had to believe in herself, not make other people believe.

"Well you've got five years to find out." His walkie talkie two-way radio buzzed and a woman's voice came through the line. Mr. Chauffeur replied.

Aileen leaned back against the bench and closed her eyes. Her flight had been early this morning. She was tired but could never sleep while travelling. She went over her high school coach's instructions for training. They usually planned a hard workout for Fridays so she could take Saturday easy.

He hadn't been impressed with her decision to use her last recruiting trip on U of G and made today's workout tougher than usual. When she moaned about it, his only sympathy came by saying she could do the workout Saturday instead. She still had to do it.

It sucked having to call the coach here in Gatica the day before she left and ask if she would be able to use the weight room and possibly the track. At least Coach Anderson had been totally understanding and said it wouldn't be a problem. With the track meet tomorrow she could use it today or possibly early tomorrow morning.

Guess it all depended on what she would be doing on the trip. She didn't think tonight would be late. The athletes had their meet tomorrow. Doing the workout in the morning seemed easier than trying to squeeze it in today. Coach Anderson had mentioned a campus tour today before practice at three o'clock.

She peeked at her watch. If the chauffeur drove at least the speed limit, they would arrive just before lunch.

"Did you know we have a good hurdler here already?" The chauffeur turned the radio down and looked at her in the review mirror.

Aileen blinked and ran the question over in her head. She thought she knew who all the hurdlers were. Gatica had a good multi eventer who could hurdle, but no strong female sprint hurdlers. "Who?"

"Tyler Jensen." He nodded. "That boy's extremely talented. Athletically, and I read in the paper the other day he's up for making the dean's list in academics. He's taking some kind of sport major."

She nodded. She knew exactly who Tyler Jensen was. His beautiful, chiselled face graced the cover of the track brochure and his long, muscular body hovered over a hurdle on the inside.

He had these amazing coloured eyes. They looked green, or blue, or grey. She couldn't decide from the picture or from the times she had watched him race this summer.

They had both competed at nationals. She was a nobody junior and he the NCAA champion. She had watched all his races at nationals and felt his disappointment when he finished fourth in the finals. It was a good, clean race until the last hurdle when he stumbled slightly and lost a placing from it. Third would have meant a trip to the World Championships.

She didn't even make the finals. She came ninth, one place away from the finals. Last summer she turned eighteen while at nationals. Her mom and dad had come to watch her race and taken her out for ice cream afterwards. She hadn't cared, two weeks before she had placed fourth at junior nationals and missed making the Can-Am international meet.

Tyler was over nineteen so he hadn't competed at the junior nationals. It wasn't until the meet in California she had noticed how cute he was. He had the perfect tan, the kind of skin that never faded in the winter. His dark hair was cropped short. It all brought out those eyes. You could notice them from the finish line, a hundred and ten meters away from where he stood before his starting blocks.

They had never spoken to each other. She ran one more race last season and blew everyone away, beating the national champion and world bronze medalist. Her time was a hundredth off the American junior record and the tenth fastest time in the world that summer.

Now she had every school in the country recruiting her, sending brochures, letters and phone calls every night. She had gone on four trips and picked Gatica as her last trip.

"Have you ever seen Tyler race?"

Aileen smiled and leaned forward in her seat. She didn't mind talking about Tyler Jensen. She just couldn't refer to him as

Tyler... yet. "I watched him this summer at nationals. He just missed out on a medal."

The driver nodded. "He was probably burnt out. Between football and then winning NCAAs in track, he probably had nothing left in the tank by the end of July."

"Good point. " She hadn't thought about that. She knew he played football because the brochure boasted about some medal or award he had won. She wasn't a football fanatic. Her cousin said it would all change when she started university and got into college football. She highly doubted it, except if she was here in Gatica, then she would watch every game. It wasn't going to happen though. She had pretty much told Stanford she would be there in September.

"So you've never been to Gatica?"

She shook her head. "I've only been to New York once. My parents and I went on holiday to Niagara Falls one time."

"Niagara Falls is nice. It's about three hours from here."

He chatted on about other great places to see in New York and the restaurants she needed to try while in Gatica. Before long he was pulling the van off the highway.

"We're about ten minutes from the school. I'll drop you off right in front of Wavertree Fieldhouse. The track offices are to the right of the main entrance on the first floor. You'll have no problem finding them."

Butterflies began wiping around in Aileen's stomach. She pulled her make-up bag out of her backpack and slipped on some lip gloss and then deodorant when the drive wasn't looking. She hoped her hair looked okay. She had straightened it last night and then stuck it in a ponytail this morning. The pony had come out a few times as she tried to keep it straight and neat. Her blonde hair preferred to have a mind of its own so she usually lived with a pony and hairband to keep the frizzes in check.

Forest trees cut away to houses. Total college town.

"I'll take you through Campus Corner."

"Campus Corner?" Aileen tried to remember if she had read about it and couldn't recall.

"It's the strip where the college kids hang out. Restaurants, shops, bars, all the things you kids need for a proper college experience." He chuckled. "If you live on this side of campus, it's walking distance."

He turned the van left and then right.

Aileen looked out the window. Little shops and restaurants had the Gatica symbol. An old movie theater had been renovated into a bar named "The Red Coats" and had an army of soldiers painted on the front of the building.

"That's where all the sport kids hang out." The driver told her about other places and when he came to a stop sign he pointed to his right. "Here's the entrance to U of G. It's the original signed from eighteen seventy-six. They've repainted the soldier but the horse and soldier monument where erected when the school opened."

A larger than life monument stood beside a stone with University of Gatica 1876 engraved in it. The monument was made of brass or copper or something that had turned green over time but the soldier's coat and hat were painted a bright, poppy red.

Aileen smiled. It was awesome!

The campus was built out of the same stone as the plaque at the front. Maybe limestone or something like that. The buildings each had vintage character to them but with a twist of the twenty-first century. She imagined walking around the campus in fall would be amazing. Even the light layer of snow covering the ground now added to the picturesque seen.

They drove by the outdoor track stadium. Someone had shovelled the two inside lanes and the mondo red track stood out bright against the snow. Behind the track was a building that looked like something that held airplanes. It had to be the indoor track – Wavertree Fieldhouse.

Aileen zipped up her coat and took a deep breath as the van pulled around and stopped in front of the building.

Here we go.

End of Excerpt

Heart of the Battle Series
Celtic Viking
Book 1
Celtic Rune
Book 2
Celtic Mann
Book 3

Coming June 2015

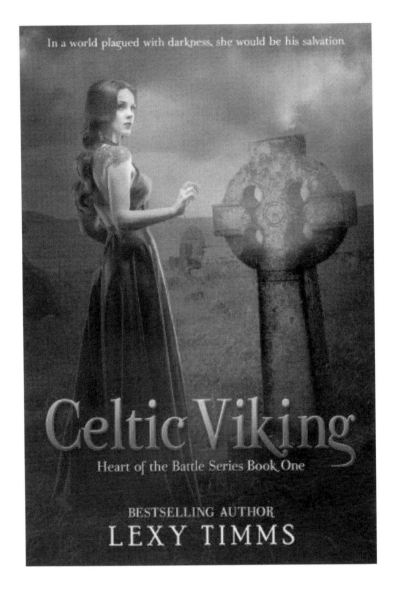

In a world plagued with darkness, she would be his salvation.

Celtic Viking

Heart of the Battle Series Book One

BESTSELLING AUTHOR
LEXY TIMMS

Did you love *Celtic Viking*? Then you should read *The Recruiting Trip* by Lexy Timms!

Aspiring college athlete Aileen Nessa is finding the recruiting process beyond daunting. Being ranked #10 in the world for the 100m hurdles at the age of eighteen is not a fluke, even though she believes that one race, where everything clicked magically together, might be. American universities don't seem to think so. Letter are pouring in from all over the country. As she faces the challenge of differentiating between a college's genuine commitment to her or just empty promises from talent-seeking coaches, Aileen heads to Gatica State University, a Division One school, on a recruiting trip. The university's athletic program boasts one of the top sprint coaches in the country. The beautiful old buildings on campus and Ivy League smarts seem so above her little Ohio town upbringing. Tyler Jensen is the school's NCAA champion in the hurdles and Jim Thorpe recipient for top defensive back in football. His incredible ocean blue eyes and confident smile make Aileen forget why she is visiting UofG. His offer to take her under his wing, should she choose to come to Gatica, is a tempting proposition that has her wondering if she might be making a deal with an angel or the devil himself.

*This is NOT erotica. It is a new adult & college Sport Romance. For Mature readers only. There are sexual situations, but no graphic sex.

Also by Lexy Timms

Hades' Spawn Motorcycle Club
One You Can't Forget
One That Got Away

Heart of the Battle Series
Celtic Viking
Celtic Rune
Celtic Mann

Managing the Bosses Series
The Boss

Saving Forever
Saving Forever - Part 1
Saving Forever - Part 2
Saving Forever - Part 3
Saving Forever - Part 4
Saving Forever - Part 5
Saving Forever - Part 6

Southern Romance Series
Little Love Affair
Siege of the Heart
Freedom Forever
Soldier's Fortune

The University of Gatica Series
The Recruiting Trip
Faster
Higher

Stronger

Standalone
Wash
Loving Charity
Summer Lovin'
Love & College
Billionaire Heart
First Love

Made in the USA
San Bernardino, CA
27 September 2015